I0587754

good deed rain

Books by Allen Frost

Ohio Trio
Bowl of Water
Another Life
Home Recordings
The Mermaid Translation
The Selected Correspondence of Kenneth
Patchen
The Wonderful Stupid Man
Saint Lemonade
Playground
Roosevelt
5 Novels
The Sylvan Moore Show
Town in a Cloud
A Flutter of Birds Passing Through Heaven:
A Tribute to Robert Sund
At the Edge of America
Lake Erie Submarine
The Book of Ticks
I Can Only Imagine
The Orphanage of Abandoned Teenagers
Different Planet
Go with the Flow: A Tribute to Clyde Sanborn
Homeless Sutra

homeless sutra

Allen Frost

Homeless Sutra ©2018
Allen Frost, Good Deed Rain
Bellingham, Washington
ISBN 978-1-64204-540-6

Writing: Allen Frost
Cover paintings: Laura Vasyutynska
Chapter illustrations: Allen Frost
Technical advice: Fred Sodt
Apple: TFK!
Cover production: Katrina Svoboda Johnson

Quotation from:
The Cloud Men of Yamato: Being an Outline of Mysticism in Japanese Literature, by E.V. Gatenby, E.P. Dutton, NY, 1929

for Clyde

homeless sutra

HOMELESS SUTRA:

Homeless Sutra......................p.10
Mountain Temple..................p.92
Instant Crow..................…......p.110
Simple Minded Sunshine...…......p.134

INTRODUCTION

Writing this collection became my companion while I also worked on Clyde Sanborn's tribute, *Go with the Flow*. Clyde was close by during this time and sometimes it felt like I could open the window and see him floating there.

HOMELESS SUTRA

PART 1:

It was a quiet gray morning. The sun hid in low clouds and Sylvan Moore told his driver, "I'll be right back."

"Yes sir," Chives replied. His usual chauffer's uniform was replaced by a plaid shirt and jeans, crowned by a blue baseball cap. Sylvan wanted to look ordinary as possible. Even their car was not the usual stretch Lincoln limousine—it was a $500 Chevette from a car lot, bought specifically for this operation. Chives kept the motor running. He was afraid it might not start again.

On the sidewalk, Sylvan looked both ways then hurried down the path towards a haunted looking house. The trench coat flapped tan sails around him. He could have been some weird prehistoric bird diving back to its roost.

No lights were on in the house. For that, Chives was glad, but he held his breath as Sylvan crept onto the porch.

A Saturday not long after dawn, there wasn't much reason for anybody to be up. The blue Chevette did fit right in, parked along a curb with others like it, in a poor neighborhood where the fantasy world of Sylvan Moore was delivered nightly to the crooked TV antennas on their roofs. In this still sleeping background, he visited like a dream.

Sylvan wasn't sure where to put the envelope full of money though. Violet Johnson's porch was crowded with worn toys, a few plastic chairs, plants begging for water, and there were fierce holes in the broken floorboards. A blue inflatable swimming pool held a green pond. He looked around and around.

Chives shook his head and covered his eyes with a camera. The car engine whined and chittered.

Finally Sylvan noticed the rusted mail slot on the front door. It squeaked as he opened the slot and jammed the thick envelope in the gap. It was stuck. But even worse than that was the sudden barking of a shrill little dog. The sound of it shot like a rocket hitting the door and Sylvan felt its hot breath on his fingertips as it pulled the envelope.

Sylvan gave one last push. The slat clacked shut as he turned and ran from the noise.

After Chives drove Sylvan home, he parked

the Chevette in the garage. He looked around nervously then he went to the backyard. It was a big field that turned into a patch of woods and finally a stone wall. He stopped near the hedge when he heard a noise.

"Over here!"

Chives reached into his jacket and took out a camera.

The man held out his hand and Chives passed it to him. "It's all on film," Chives said.

"We'll take a look at it."

"Err, excuse me," Chives said, "I believe we settled on a price."

The man laughed. "We'll see about that."

Two hours later, it hit the news. Sylvan's assistant Artie Kahn nearly dropped the portable TV off his lap. "Boss!" he choked. "You're not going to like this."

No, he didn't. And the network didn't like it either. The news was like a wildfire and the rest of the morning and well into the afternoon, Sylvan was shuttled back and forth between meeting rooms. He was programmed like a talking toy and when he went on the stage, surrounded by corporate reporters, he knew how to respond. Sylvan stood at the podium graceful as a blue heron and projected that calm warmth everyone knew from his evening TV show. It seemed to go well. Honestly, behind all the words and bright lights, Sylvan thought he did alright, but at 3 o'clock, his old friend Bert Neebers told him they would have to let him go. That was it.

It wasn't just Violet Johnson. There was a string of other losing contestants Sylvan gave money to. He had been doing it for at least a year. Maybe more. No wonder the network had to fire him. His actions went against the fundamental premise of *Winners & Losers*.

Two cars drove him home from the studio. Sylvan sat alone in the backseat following the first car, filled with the contents of his office—boxes full of awards, plaques and trophies that had lined the shelves and walls. None of it meant anything anymore.

When he arrived at the end of his winding driveway, his limousine was gone. Chives took it. The big house awaited him silently. How quickly everything became a sand castle.

The driver of the car in front was already unloading the cardboard boxes onto the ground as Sylvan left his car. A breeze made the tall poplar trees seem to breathe.

Sylvan watched the last box clack on top of the stack and without another word, the driver got back into his car. Like clockwork, the two cars left together.

Birds sang in the leaves.

Violet was stopped at the bank. Her dog shredded all that money someone stuffed in her house. She spent most of the day taping the bills together, but it didn't matter—the bank turned it over as evidence for the case against Sylvan Moore. Violet Johnson sighed. She lost again. She watched them take it away.

The sun sat on the edge of the stone wall like a pumpkin.

Sylvan Moore was in his backyard, ignoring the phone and television. Those cardboard boxes made the journey outside with him. They were empty now. All the gold awards lay scattered at the bottom of the pool and Sylvan brooded with his legs in the water. He could easily slip off the ledge and sink to the treasures twelve feet below. There was nothing left to throw in but him. That wasn't his intention though. He wasn't done. He was thinking about Violet Johnson.

Before taping every program, he would introduce himself to each of the contestants and listen to their story. Then when the cameras were rolling, he would have a little something personal to tell the viewers about tonight's guests. That was one of the few creative things he got to do, besides the occasional wisecrack, impression, or aside. He liked to find that one little spark in each person that made them special: The shoe salesman from Topeka who married the wrong twin. The woman who had been struck by lightning three times. The police officer who arrested a horse. Everyone had some entertaining account. The challenge for Sylvan was those people who seemed to barely make it through each day, the ones whose suffering gave them little to say: "I'm a divorced office worker with bills to pay." There seemed to be a lot of people that way. And then there was Violet Johnson.

Even in the bright light of the studio, she was pale. Her eyes were hollows, dark pools that showed no sign of seeing the way out. Anytime she spoke, her hands trembled near her mouth as if she was reluctant to let the words go. And as the game progressed, Sylvan felt more and more sorry to hear her answers. They were always wrong. She finished the game at dead last, she hadn't made a cent.

And worst of all, she looked like she expected that would happen. That was the moment Sylvan Moore decided he had to help her.

His tapping foot made ripples across the pool.

A lot happened since the early morning.

It must have been a slow news day for the rest of the world. Sylvan Moore was the leading story every radio hour, and the TV ran live reports. What was Sylvan Moore doing secretly giving money away? The evening newspaper headlines ran **Moore's Mad Money** in bold.

By then Sylvan Moore had been forced

inside. There were helicopters overhead.

Early the next morning before the photographers and journalists could surround his door, Sylvan Moore started the Chevette and backed out of the garage.

He followed the track of the driveway with the headlights off. A big full moon lit the way.

It was nearly the exact scene as the morning before, with the Chevette creeping across the grounds, only now Chives was gone and Sylvan was driving himself.

He pressed the button on the controller and the gates opened. He was a little surprised no dim shadows leaped out of the way, flashing cameras at him as he passed through. Maybe his story had already run its course, maybe something flashier had taken his place? In any case, the last day changed Sylvan Moore. He no longer had his show, and he was leaving his mansion for good. He didn't know what would happen next.

PART 2

It was still hard not to hear his name on the radio. As he turned the dial, going from song to song. He was hours from the city, but it seemed he hadn't got away. He was stopped at the edge of a huge parking lot. It stretched like a dark ocean. To his left was the street leading back to the highway; to his right, across the acre of asphalt, was Mammoth Mart. People flocked to it like a holy site. Sylvan had a bag of apples, a jar of jam, and a loaf of bread on the backseat. Once he was in that store, he didn't know what else to get. He was worried he would be recognized and he hurried back to his car. It was okay though—people in the everyday world don't expect to see stars.

Sylvan turned the radio off and rolled the window down. He listened to the afternoon, heard a train rumble, horn somewhere unseen. Cars went by on the street. Everywhere there were wheels.

Funny, this was the first time he had been alone like this in years—no crew, no Artie Kahn trailing him, no loud music, white lights, applause...And no Diana Bright. No Chives either...Sylvan sat in the driver's seat, in charge of where he would go.

He still wasn't there yet.

The key turned in his hand and the car started again. Moving slowly along the edge of the tar it didn't go very far, just to the corner of the lot where a phone booth stood. It was bright, like a lighthouse, reflecting the sunshine of the day.

Sylvan opened the car door and got out. He still wore his sunglasses and down jacket with the collar turned up. That was his disguise. People were used to him wearing a suit. Cars going by would just see another weird looking guy.

The phone booth didn't look like it got many visitors. Inside was filled with the sound of a sigh, the air in there captured 1988.

Sylvan lifted the plastic receiver off its cradle and heard a hum. He put three quarters in the slot. The sound of them rattled and clinked the machinery. The Sylvan dialed a number he knew by heart.

After two rings, a woman answered and he spoke to her.

"Hello, Diana."

"Sylvan!"

"Hi."

"Where are you, Sylvan?"

He caught the start of a desperate laugh against his hand. "Some little town," he said. He couldn't see much of it through the cracked glass. A couple gas stations and fast food signs on the road. He knew it would be hard to talk to Diana Bright, but he couldn't leave without letting her know.

"Are you okay?"

He said, "Sure. Everything's fine. I'm just stepping away for a while."

"I've been trying to call you," she said. "The news is terrible. They're saying so many awful things."

"Yes." Sylvan took a breath. "Well, you know me, right? You know what to believe."

"Oh, Sylvan." That sound made him wish he held her.

"Don't worry," was all he had left to say. With a sudden loud clink, the connection was cut. Seventy five cent didn't buy much.

He cradled the receiver and stepped out of the booth. Poor Diana. She had been the beautiful smiler on his TV show for thirty years. He stared at the blue sky.

He knew Diana wouldn't tell about him— she was understanding and forgiving. She always was. He wished he had been more like her. He wished he had asked how she was doing now.

Hard to believe everything was over, just like that.

In the late afternoon he found the perfect spot. Off the road, a narrow dirt clearing led into a thicket. The Chevette crawled in there like a beetle and stopped. It was just where Sylvan wanted to be, hidden from traffic, with the ocean not far away.

How much time passed with him just sitting there? Only a minute. But Sylvan was new to this kind of quiet.

A chickadee hopped on a thin branch of snowberry. The blue car hood reflected all the leaves like a still pond. How long, he wondered, would it take for him to be forgotten?

He followed a path, no more than a deer trail really, that took him from the bracken onto bare sloping rock. A short cliff fell the rest of the way into the water. Sylvan sat on a mossy stone and watched the motion of the high tide. Back and forth, the water came and went. Wasn't it all the working of the moon that made the ocean breathe like that? It had been a long time since Sylvan sat in a Nebraska classroom learning about the world. What a long climb from there to the top, to this rock where he watched the clockwork rise and fall, sizzle and sigh.

He saw a purple starfish beneath the surge. Just like him, it was stuck to a stone too. Sylvan wasn't pleased when that thought crept into his mind. Surely he was more than a starfish. He diverted his eyes to the distant waves. The sun sparked among them. Then he looked back. Did that starfish have a TV show that reached out to millions? He glared at it. Like a purple hand, it held to the barnacle covered rock underwater. What had that starfish achieved? Not fame, not wealth, it didn't live in a mansion. It clung to a rock while the waves washed over it. It didn't have anything. It just was.

Sylvan looked back out to sea.

He had not always been the person he now seemed to be. There were plenty of things he had done he felt terrible about. His memory took him right back in time. Winners & Losers would go on location to other cities around the country: Tampa, Chicago, Phoenix, Boulder, and others. Sylvan looked forward to this travel, the company jet, the first class hotels, and the excitement of the crowd. It must have been that phone call today that made him remember Seattle. He was in a foul mood about something, looking out the oval window as their jet descended. Diana Bright was in the plush seat across the aisle and as usual she was all smiles. He snapped at her, "What do you like so much about Seattle?" She said, "I like the outdoors. I like the mountains, the trees and water." And Sylvan muttered, "Oh brother." He stayed that way, smoldering, until they got to the waiting limousine. Chives had loaded their bags and Sylvan stepped in front of Diana, "This is my limo," he said and added, "Didn't you say you like the outdoors?" Then he got in, sat alone on the wide backseat and told Chives to go. That was years ago, but did that sound like the same person who would give Violet Johnson fifty grand?

With a sigh, Sylvan came back to the present. Night was on the way. His seat lay flat and he stared at the car ceiling. He thought sleeping like this would be easy, with his blanket pulled up to his chin all he would have to do is close his eyes. But it was uncomfortable.

He couldn't quite stretch his legs out and his thoughts jumped about wildly like laundry strung in the wind. He wondered at every little sound outside. It got darker, but his eyes stayed open.

Much as he liked the Chevette for its ability to slip into the leaves, Sylvan wished he chose something bigger to sleep in. He was all aches, cold and tired and finally he resolved to get out of the car into the new blue light of dawn.

He opened the door and pulled himself out. Sleeping in a car—his legs felt like they had been pulled off, mangled, and screwed back on backwards. He rubbed his sore hips with his knuckles and looked around. A few birds tapped about on branches. There was dew on the car, making it gleam. Seagulls in the distance. The air was cold and clear as a glass of water.

Sylvan stamped his feet on the path. He thought of going to the shore to throw a handful of ocean on his face. Hard to believe that yesterday he woke in a bed and rang Chives for breakfast. Was it a mistake to have gone to Violet's house after that? Would he do it over again? Wasn't it all just waiting to happen? Sooner or later, this morning would occur. The moment he found sympathy for the losers on his show he couldn't be a part of his old world any longer.

PART 3

Sylvan lived in that little hidden spot for three days. He had a routine. He would go to the shore in the morning. His last morning there, he sat on his usual rock. His favorite starfish had wandered off—he should have seen that as an omen.

But he just watched the water. Yesterday he saw a tanker or freighter on the horizon. After an hour, he returned to his car. The window in back was broken. Diamonds of glass littered the ground.

His bag of groceries was missing from the seat. Someone tore through his car in a hurry. There wasn't much to begin with and even less now.

How could somebody do this? he kept thinking. He swept glass off the back seat with a cedar branch. He put scraps of paper back in the glovebox. A crumpled map. The radio was gone. They pried it out of the dashboard.

Sylvan did the best he could putting the car in order, then he had to sit down. How could somebody do this? He had to stop thinking that. He sat on the front bumper and took a deep breath of the trees and ragged leaves around him.

The song had started again—the breeze, the birds here and there, the low hush of the ocean. It was comforting as a lullaby, but it was time to go.

At least the thief didn't take the steering wheel. Or the windshield, or the view out the glass. The world was painted before him.

With no radio anymore, the new music came from the broken window in back. A rush of cold air, the sound of the tires and roar of speed. When he stopped again he would think of a way to stop that noise. Some cardboard and tape would do for the time being.

He couldn't help wondering, if the radio was there would he still hear them talking about him? Maybe it was good the radio was gone. That broken sound of the wind said it all.

That map was in the glovebox but Sylvan was gone from its straight lines and names. He was following little roads that could run out of tar, cough into gravel, slow down into dirt and fir needles. He was looking for the great alone, where you leave everything behind.

Roads are rivers. He stopped the car when he found its source. He couldn't go any further. Surrounded by trees, with a big mountain in the distance, he braked and turned the engine off. To his right where a stream ran, he heard a heron croak and take off into the air. Sylvan waited until all he could hear was the burbling water, then he opened the door and stepped outside.

A wave seemed to pass through him. He caught the Chevette roof trim and swayed as the wave left him. Hunger. His food was all gone. For a moment the stream talked to him like the radio. What did it say? What language was it? He couldn't tell—not in the daytime—not yet.

Water. It was funny how he always had to be near it. When he left the pool at his house with his sunken awards and trophies, the place he ran to was the ocean. Now, at the end of the road, he found this shallow river. He left his car and went to it.

A cedar tree let him lean and look. It was a perfect spot. A wide streambed, twenty yards across, paved with round river rocks. Out in the middle snaked the green shining current. He supposed that salmon were born along here and found their way back when they were old. They came from the ocean just like him. Sylvan slid down along the trunk and sat. He thought of a salmon, felt the cold water of the ocean and could hear off in the distance the chanting song of the river calling him home.

On his show, Sylvan used to kid the Number One camera. "Are you getting this, Carol?" he would ask and behind the camera lens, she would make the camera slowly nod. It was a gag they used for years. And who had not heard someone say that catchphrase out in the day-to-day world? A Sylvan Moore echo. Only now, it was hard to imagine Carol with her nodding camera. The sun and moon came and went. Sylvan was wrapped in a blanket with a broad leaf on his head. Dotted with the starting raindrops, he sat silently and breathed. Carol would have stared at him until the film ran out.

Sylvan was a new creature to the woods, one that moved very little, only to forage for some berries or leaves, or pull roots from the ground, then back to his cedar tree. Birds would hop around where he sat. A snail with a whirling shell crawled over his foot on its slow way to somewhere else. The world around him made trails, even the sounds in the air spread like the branches of trees.

When he stood up, he moved through layers.

He felt rain on his hand. Weakly, he pulled the blanket tighter and watched his feet take steps. Going back and forth to the river had made a path, pushed down weeds and pressed the memory of him into the ground. Even the stones in the riverbed were familiar to him, watching him drifting like a ghost on his way to the water.

The rain was picking up but it felt alright. It made spots on the rocks. In a while the dry riverbed would shine with colors. There would be sky-blue stones, red, black, white and those ones green as jade.

Sylvan had a rock he liked to sit on, right by the water's edge. It was smooth dark gray, like a whale just breaking through the ice.

He dipped his hand in the swift current and tasted the mountain. It was so cold it ran through his empty body all the way to his toes.

As he sat on the whale's back, he caught motion in the thick leaves on the other bank. He watched as a deer appeared.

It knew the rocks as well as he did, passing over them quickly, never taking eyes off of Sylvan. By this time Sylvan was no stranger to the deer. They walked around him with no fear.

This one though was nearly running. A rock clattered into the stream when the deer stopped only twenty feet from Sylvan. Its sides bellowed as it breathed, deeply, mouth open, closed, open.

Sylvan swore it was trying to speak. Could that be? Of course, he told himself, Everything in the world has changed.

"What is it?" Sylvan asked.

The deer wanted to talk. If huffed twice, loud, making clouds.

Sylvan closed his eyes. He couldn't believe what he was seeing. When he opened them, the deer was gone. There was a moment of quiet and then the river roared. It seemed to stand up out of the rocks like a wall. From upstream came the thunder of more. The flashflood hit Sylvan, grabbed him and ripped him along.

Wars were still being fought, there were plagues that couldn't be stopped, fears sold newspapers, and fresh every week, TV and radio chatter moved on to other matters, some other outrage of another politician or celebrity caught in the spotlight. Sylvan Moore was forgotten after a month or so.

Where was he? What was his story? All that water that rolled and pummeled him carried him far downstream to a sandbar. Wouldn't that have made a picture for the papers? Imagine how that would have played.

Instead, he was found by a man and his dog. They brought Sylvan to a camper truck. It had a bed and a kitchen and a table with books. There was a woodstove the man kept refueled so the little house on wheels stayed warm. Slowly, after several days, Sylvan could do more than just eat a little soup and bread, stare at the owl feather tied to the window frame, and sleep.

"You're looking much better this morning," the man said.

Sylvan could smell coffee.

The man moved from the stove and sat near his dog. It was a big poodle. Sylvan knew the feel of its wet nose and tongue.

Sylvan took a breath and asked, "Where am I?"

"Alive," the man said. "Charley and I have been taking care of you." He poured two cups full of coffee.

That was the morning Sylvan's thoughts flocked back together. He could sit up, he could move again. He followed the man and Charley outside to the shore where they first found him.

The river was wide and filled with rain and all that ice dislodged from the mountain. It wasn't the same little stream you could almost leap over. It boiled along with fast green churning current. Sylvan though of all those stones, all those faces, underwater.

Later that afternoon, Sylvan said goodbye to the man and his dog. He walked upstream along the shore towards the white mountain.

Crumpled in his hand was a paper bag the man gave him. It held a sandwich and an apple. Sylvan felt like he was going off to school, or his first job at the radio station. The man also drew a map on the crinkled brown paper. The man and his dog had been everywhere in their truck and the directions would get Sylvan where he needed to be. He was okay with that. He was just a stick fallen in the river, going wherever he was guided. First he had to find where he left his car.

PART 4

Sylvan braked and stopped. The road forked. The arrow pointing left was painted TOWN. The other arrow pointing right was blank, unpainted wood. This was exactly what the paper bag map showed he would find. He didn't have to give it a second thought. He turned the wheel and drove on.

Around the next corner, the road was tarred and the sun shined on a meadow. It was a bright green clearing in the middle of the trees. He could see a pond too. Blackbirds flew about it.

Another moment and he was back in the woods. Big fir trees made it dark on either side and autumn colored maple trees stretched branches over the road. Orange and yellow leaves skated down from the heights. They covered the road and scurried as the car drove over them.

Sylvan had no idea where he was going.

The map on the paper bag ended with the signpost drawing. "Follow that road," was all the man told him. That was all he had to know.

The leaves reminded Sylvan that winter was on the way. The nights were getting colder. Sleeping outside, or in a car would be rougher.

He hoped he was headed somewhere warmer. He smiled as he thought of the TV show. Sometimes a contestant would be losing and then with a lucky spin, the wheel would land them on a trip to Mexico or some tropical island dream. That could happen to me, Sylvan thought, you never know. Hoping helps, but he was okay with where he was. He was safe, he had his next meal taken care of. What more did he need?

For a moment he swore he heard music. He glanced at the space the radio left behind. He had to be hearing things. He was too far from people, it was quiet as a fairytale woods.

Sylvan turned to look over his shoulder. The car wasn't loud enough to have a broken window, was it? "What?!" he squawked. Does that make sense? The only sound was the tinny whine of the engine and the window in back had been repaired. Sometimes when things happen, you don't ask why or why not.

He looked back at the road in time to brake and take a sharp turn.

The Chevette purred down a hill winding out of the trees. Sylvan was surprised to find the forest gone so suddenly. The road leveled out in a valley, with fields on either side.

He had to squint to make out the crop. Pumpkins.

For another five minutes, he seemed to drive through a shallow orange ocean. Sylvan had never seen so many pumpkins. Who needed that many? They glowed and glowed until the road slowed five minutes later.

A smooth river flowed in front of him. A signpost arrow pointed the way for Sylvan to go next, following along the piled embankment of that swift water.

He glanced in the rearview mirror at his orange wake, another strange world left behind him.

He turned the steering wheel. There was no traffic headed his way and he let the Chevette ease onto the riverside road.

A big willow passed.

Sylvan admired the grassy bed beneath the umbrella of its long green leaves. What a nice place to live, with the water for your door and a tree for your roof. He tucked the thought away.

In simple perspective, the road stretched across the flat in front of him—pumpkin fields on his right, the river on his left, a big gray sky overhead.

An eagle passed low over the telephone wires. It carried a branch in its claws, dragging it through the air like a crayon. You could follow it to a big scribble of branches way up in a poplar tree.

Sylvan pictured the man and his dog driving through here. Would he have stopped his green truck beside the river, found a spot on the steep slope to throw a stick in the water for Charley?

It was almost too easy to let the car drive itself on the flat straightaway while he looked at the river flow. But the next time he glanced ahead of him, Sylvan saw someone leaning from the field, holding an arm out into the road.

It was the first person Sylvan had seen in a while. Somebody hitchhiking. Sylvan slowed.

The town just suddenly crept out of the ground. Sylvan couldn't see the river anymore, it was hidden behind buildings and signs and trees. He had a funny thought, wondering if someone had planted seeds for houses, gas stations, the grocery, post office and all the little stores lined in a row along Main Street. "Is this where you wanted to go?" Sylvan asked his passenger in the backseat.

Not surprisingly, it was quiet in the car.

Sylvan parked beside the curb where there was a nice bench and a blue mailbox. It was a good spot for someone to wait for something to happen. He got out and went to the Chevette's back door.

His passenger needed help getting out, but at least he was light. The hitchhiker, stuffed with straw, was a scarecrow.

Sylvan settled him on the bench and was pleased to see the scarecrow looked quite comfortable in his spot. Sylvan propped the arm along the back of the bench and took a step back. "I'll see you later." Sylvan gave him what he thought was a last wave and went back to his car.

The engine started right up, but Sylvan sat at the wheel staring ahead. Where was he supposed to go? Why was he even here? All because of that man and his dog who found him in a flashflood stream and brought him back from the dead…Well, he supposed, if he was to be here, he ought to look around.

A big truck grumbled past, flatbed filled with pumpkins.

The Chevette followed it hesitantly, brake lights glowing, then turned on a side street towards the river.

With a soft plop, the scarecrow's arm dropped to his side.

Sylvan Moore was not used to this new life. From having everything, with all his needs cared to and every moment accounted for, he was now adrift. He was letting go and learning as he went.

When he finished his sandwich, he sat for a while, staring at the brick patterns on the wall next to the car. With nothing to do, what were you supposed to do?

He went for a walk.

After his time in the woods it was strange to be in the midst of everything created by people. They had worked hard to cover the ground with tar and concrete and buildings. He didn't know what a deer would think of it, but he was starting to like the old wooden buildings, the gothic-looking windows in the eaves on the second floors above the stores, the lampposts, the brick alleys, sidewalks, the flower shop, the skeins of electric wires overhead, and behind it all ran the river.

Something else he noticed—the town really took pumpkins seriously. In nearly every window, on flags, bumper stickers, even graffiti… He guessed that's what the town was known for. Anyway, it was hard to escape their presence. Pumpkins were everywhere.

When the street he was on ran out of shops and walls and turned into a road leading into green fir trees and the low hills in the distance, Sylvan turned and walked towards the water. The afternoon sky was darkening, it would be good to find somewhere to sleep before the night began.

He crossed a gravel lot and found a trail cutting along the riverbank. The current was moving along with him. A couple small, silver motorboats were returning to town. They moved slow and low, filled with a catch of ripe pumpkins. Ahead of Sylvan, stairs kneeled down to docks where other boats like them were tied up. The throb of the outboards approached, a seagull crying above, and as they passed him, the waves broke on the shore.

PART 5

Sylvan tucked his legs up tight, knees pressed to the door, trying to stay warm with only one blanket and his other clothes piled on top. He didn't think about once upon a time, the mansion, the comfort, the softness of other nights. He wasn't there anymore.

The Chevette wasn't meant to be slept in. His sore, stressed bones and muscles wanted to leap right out of him and march away. They wouldn't stop until they reached where he used to be. Wouldn't that be a sight, lounging by the pool? And where would that leave what was left of him? Wait until that gruesome sight was discovered in an abandoned car that once belonged to a disgraced TV personality…

Sylvan stretched his legs again and lay flat on his back. He stared at the gloomy ceiling. Another day was on the way. Rain drops tapped the roof.

It was a nice sound, like the sound of tiny hands. He shut his eyes and listened to the clapping. Sylvan knew that audience sound from his days on the stage, but he also knew it wasn't just for him. All around town, they were gathered, watching over everyone.

Seven nights and days of rain flowed over him. He was used to the feeling, used to the routine when in the morning he opened the car door and stuck his legs out.

He lived close to the river. He could see it through a gap in the blackberry bramble. Sort of like a fairytale, he found this perfect spot to park, nearly surrounded by vines and thorns and withered leaves. He snuck the Chevette in next to an old wooden boat up on blocks. Blue paint worn from its hull. The rain was its only taste of riding on water.

Sylvan stood and shut the car door. After that clang, he zipped his coat, put his hands in his pockets and started to walk.

Once out of the thicket, he tipped his head back to face the falling rain. It wasn't the same as taking a hot shower, but it was free, straight from the clouds. Each drop that found him fell for miles. It made you appreciate water. Wasn't it all one big wheel? Sylvan remembered that Nebraska school. The cycle of rain, fog, hail, snow, feeding the ground, the seeds and rivers running to the ocean, evaporating, forming clouds and starting again.

The dirt parking lot he stood on was turning to mud.

He was dizzy and held his arms out flat like wings to keep from landing in the muck. He might not have the strength to get up. He might flow like that runneled dirty water off to the river on its way to the sea, on its way to become clouds and rain once again.

Like a heron, he folded his outspread arms back to his sides, pushed his hands in coat pockets and took big steps to avoid puddles.

He made it to the eaves of the warehouse and slid along the wall. The water overflowed from the gutter and rang splattering on the chips of stone at his feet.

Getting wet was just part of living this way. He surprised a sparrow as he turned the corner. A bird has the good sense to hide out of weather as much as possible, but even a bird has to go looking for food.

Sylvan was hungry too and cold and also very wet by the time he reached Clouds.

The café light was on behind the counter, in the kitchen. The front door was locked but Sylvan passed the glass windows, around to the alley where the delivery door was left open.

A lot had happened in the last week. The man and the dog had been right to send him here. He was getting accustomed to it. Sylvan had a table, a chair by the woodstove, with a bowl of oatmeal and hot pumpkin tea. He was also getting accustomed to pumpkin—everything had pumpkin in it. He didn't have any money, but he bet if he did it would have a big pumpkin printed on it. He didn't need money though. George the cook would make him breakfast for free. Sandy the waitress gave him a bag full of clothes and the dishwasher Nick told Sylvan about the one machine at the laundromat that didn't need coins. The everyday wanderings were free and in the evenings Sylvan would come back to Cloud for entertainment. There was always music or stories. It was better than TV. Could that be? He was starting to think so.

For a long time Sylvan sat warming his hands around the oatmeal bowl. The radio in the kitchen played. With a clacking sound, George was cutting pumpkin rhythmically.

These people were so kind to Sylvan, and what had he done? Did they know who he was? They never let on. He didn't know how recognizable he was anymore. He felt his chin.

A beard was growing there. He was a long way from a suit and shiny TV smile. After what he had been through he could never return to that person. The fire popped and crackled in the stove. George sang along with the radio as he started the soup of the day. Sylvan felt warm again.

The day wore on. The cloud layer scuffed aside and Sylvan found himself sitting by the river's edge in the sunshine.

Everything seemed to sigh with the light. The ground steamed. The weeds were bent with diamonds. Dew was everywhere.

As the last couple late fishing boats left town, Sylvan raised his hand to them.

He watched the wake, the waves, and the way the river recovered so you never knew a boat had passed by.

Seagulls tangled and cried in a halo above the docks. The boats were back. Pumpkins were unloaded onto wagons and Sylvan was lending a hand. With a rag and a bucket of river water he cleaned the mud off each orange shell. He had to work fast, it was like a pumpkin assembly line. As soon as one wagon was done, another load was pulled before him. Sometimes Sylvan had to stop so he could scoop fresh water in the bucket. A muddy cloud would be chucked in the river. His hand was numb from the cold.

A wagon went up the ramp and came back down for more. It was surprising how many pumpkins the boats had hauled to shore, but Sylvan had seen the fields outside of town. The land was covered with them. They could steer their boats along the channels and fill their hulls, come back slow and low and followed by gulls. All this had been going on for years and for an hour or so Sylvan was a part.

By the time the last cart bumped up the ramp he felt tired and sore. His clothes were cold and wet again as he knelt on the edge of the dock to wash out the bucket and cloth.

"Thanks for your help."

Sylvan turned around.

Jimmy held a pumpkin and offered it.

"Oh," Sylvan said. "Thanks." He cradled it in his left arm, his right was numb.

Jimmy said, "If you ever want to earn another one, we're here this time every day."

Sylvan nodded, "Okay." Honestly though, he didn't know what he was going to do with one pumpkin, let alone a carful from a week of work. "Thanks again."

PART 6

Sylvan carried the pumpkin along the weedy path back to his car. It wasn't far. He saw a salmon break the surface. The river had turned into a road for them as they were returning from the sea, going to those sandy beds far upstream where they were born.

His own home was waiting for him, hidden in blackberry behind a pile of old wet lumber and a forgotten boat. The morning mud had mostly dried and it was nice to catch sight of his car. The setting sun glowed a window on the ground. A couple bees hopped along the dandelions grown near the tire tracks. What a nice feeling to have a home to return to. He pictured those salmon that made it back, gliding in under the forest overgrowth, with the rocks and silt smooth below their skin and the current holding them in place.

He opened the Chevette and set the pumpkin on the floor mat. No, he still didn't know what he was supposed to do with it. Did people have bank accounts, did they store pumpkins in vaults? He would ask George in the morning. Better yet, he decided he would give it to him. He reached for a bag on the backseat and spilled out the clothes Sandy gave him. They weren't exactly warm to wear, but it was intense pleasure to put on clean clothes.

He gathered the wet clothing into a ball and left the shadows of his car. A bird scared out of the branches got quickly lost in another seam. The blackberry grew like a wall, but Sylvan had found a spot on the riverside of it where he could dry his clothes. Two branches stuck in the earth with a rope stretched between, his clothes could dry safe from sight. That was assuming another sunny day was on the way tomorrow.

Sylvan was careful to avoid the thorns as he looked for the string. Once a vine caught you, it would bite and hold on and send all its taut snakelike pull into keeping you put. It was dusk but they were just as hungry, reaching out silhouettes. Sylvan leaned around them and found his clothesline. He unwrapped his bindle and hung his shirt and pants. The rope sagged and the sticks bent but held like two old telephone poles. Would the moonlight dry them at all? he wondered. The sky was clear, no sign of clouds. The moon would do what it could.

On his way back to the car his arm did

catch a branch. He unhooked the thorns from the plaid cloth. It was amazing how quickly the winter dark spilled over everything. The pile of blackberry loomed like an unlit house.

Sylvan found the way in. It wasn't hard to find your way around in the dark when you've been there a while.

The boat gloomed up above him. Sometimes he had the urge to climb on board. It was like living next to a mountain and not going to the top. That thought made him laugh. He imagined the film cameras, lights, booms and crew to film him live on location as he broadcast from the slanted deck of that boat.

Then it was gone. He wasn't in millions of TVs anymore and he didn't want to be. There were things he could do to give back to the new world he was in. It didn't have to be a weekly gameshow—he could do far simpler things— like help with the pumpkins. How to live with other people, how to give and share with the least he ever had when he seemed all alone out here—that lesson was the most he ever learned. He held to the car as a wave seemed to go over him. He used to be outside his body, now he was in—he felt his thoughts, the cold, everything.

The wave passed. It seethed through the leaves surrounding him, moving on like a gust of wind.

Being far from electricity, the dark happened fast. Sylvan yawned. Sleep was waiting for him to get in the car. The Chevette and the boat and the bushes were just blacker shapes in the night. The only light came from the sky and something small as a planet—an orange dot projected on the car dashboard, moving unsteadily.

Sylvan was curious. He opened the door and the dot was still there. It wasn't some reflection cast off the glass; it was alive as a miniature spotlight. He followed the thin ray to the orange source on the floor. Like the world's smallest movie, he could see where the light was coming from.

The pumpkin had a nail-sized hole in its shell. As Sylvan watched, he saw another one appear, and another beam of narrow light made a new spot on the ceiling. Then he could hear it—the faintest little tapping, like a mouse with a hammer.

Another hole shot a beam of light out the window. Right on the floor of his car, the pumpkin was disintegrating like a slow motion time bomb. Sylvan wanted to pick it up and heave it into the berry. He found he was frozen though, staring as it happened. Something was poking from inside, making those holes. He caught a glimpse of a steely looking point. Whatever was doing it wasn't letting up. Soon there was a string of holes like a brightly lit necklace that ran right around the shell. The front seat of the Chevette glowed.

Sylvan didn't want to grab the pumpkin and get stabbed, but he did reach around it to clear the map away and the paper bag. The pumpkin looked like it was filled with fire.

The blade started to saw along the row of dotted lights. It wouldn't be long now. Sylvan took a step back. The top of the pumpkin was ready to blow off like the lid of a teapot.

He wished he could retreat further but the blackberries brushed at his coat.

The next moment Sylvan shut his eyes. He covered them with his hands too, but he could still see that blast of hot furnace light. He peered through his fingers.

The Chevette was lit up like a jack o' lantern.

Shading his eyes, Sylvan watched something bright as a flare burning inside the pumpkin. It hopped out and jumped around the edges like some living creature made of fire.

Sylvan froze and flickered in that crackling orange light.

The fireball looked around, saw the sky and spread out wings. It flapped them and shot by Sylvan in a blur. He tipped on one leg as it rocketed past and he almost fell watching it race and sizzle around the stars. He lost sight of it behind the thick wall of blackberry leaves. He couldn't tell if it was on its way to the moon, or sightseeing the valley at night.

After a few minutes blinking and rubbing his eyes, Sylvan could see again. The bird, or whatever it was, had left a seared image wherever he looked, but finally the black night was back.

He reached inside the car and got the saucer off the dashboard. A green candle was melted to it. Sylvan liked to read a little before he slept. He kept a book of matches in his coat pocket.

Something trickled in the blackberries. It was probably some small animal settling in.

Sylvan struck a match and lit the candle. He hoped he wouldn't see a charred floor and the remains of Cape Canaveral. That bird could have set his whole car on fire.

He lowered the candlelight. There sat the pumpkin, hollowed out, jaggedly cut where the creature had gone out through the top. The stemmed cap lay to the side like a hat fallen off. Whatever fire it burned with didn't harm the car at all.

This was one of the drawbacks to being alone—when something like this occurred, there was no one you could turn to and say, "What just happened?"

"When I got my start in show business, when I really put myself on the map, was when I was the summer replacement for Ward Cotton." Sylvan paused at the mention of his old mentor. Any other time he told this story there would be a sort of sigh of recognition for that name. Not here though. The audiences gathered around him at Clouds waited for him to continue. "Ward Cotton?" he repeated. Didn't they have TVs in this town? Or was it just this crowd? Was it before their time? The name meant nothing to them, but they watched Sylvan eagerly. "Ward Cotton was on the air, radio and television, for over forty years. Seemed like everyone in America knew him. He was an institution. Anyway, Ward was the host of *Winners & Losers*, at that time a new program. That's a sort of variety gameshow—I'm not sure if you've heard of it—it may not transmit this far…" he paused and smiled at the candlelit tables, "So every summer though, Ward likes to take a vacation. Packs up the family, the butler, the fine china, and heads out to the ocean. Naturally they want to keep the show going while he's gone—not everyone has a seaside castle and two months off work." Sylvan soaked up a little of the laughter in the room and continued, "They chose yours truly to step into those shoes. The work wasn't entirely new to me. At that point I had been on television for a few years. I even had my own show on the Blue Network. *More Sylvan*. I don't know if any of you remember that? It's alright…That was a long time ago." He took a sip of pumpkin tea.

"Anyway, it was an honor to be considered, to be handed the reins to that popular, nationally syndicated show. I did well though. I called my parents and everyone I knew. I was having fun. Honestly, I seemed to be having the time of my life. People said I was bringing humor and youthful energy. I had my own partner, Diana Bright, who the viewers loved. I would wake at 4:30 AM and work all day, coming up with new things that had never been tried on TV. By the end of the summer season there was such an outpouring of letters begging me to stay on that the network met with Ward Cotton and the old man actually announced he would be leaving the show for another assignment. I was astonished. It felt like the king just gave me the crown. *Winners & Losers* was mine. Of course at that time I had no idea what Ward Cotton felt, it would me take thirty years doing the show to know. Now I know…Then I was a young man, it was a brand new adventure. I was so excited by the attention, the life of a star. It was only about a month after I took over when my assistant Artie Kahn brought me a letter. Another fan letter, I thought." Sylvan reached for his teacup, lifted it and saw it was empty. He was almost done with the story. He knew Sandy would refill the cup when he was done talking. He held the empty cup anyway and continued.

"I was wrong. The letter said: We have been such fans of Ward Cotton. We have enjoyed his program for years. It broke our hearts to see him leave." Sylvan sighed and shook his head. The punchline had arrived and he steadied himself. Every time he told this story before, it always ended with applause and laughter. But all of a sudden he knew it was going to sound like a pretty corny joke, but chances are they wouldn't know it and anyway he was almost there. Tomorrow he could tell them a serious story. He could tell them how he got to where he was. Tomorrow.

Sylvan took a deep breath and finished it. "The letter was signed by my mother."

Does everyone arrive on this planet with a talent? Sylvan walked along the dark trail beside the river. He could hear the black water running. It was past ten but he could see his breath cloud in front of him. There was just enough light to see. It seemed to come from the atmosphere, a couple bulbs in a back lot, the haze above the silhouettes. You didn't need to travel to outer space to find yourself in another world. Sylvan had done it without a rocket.

He wasn't worried about slipping off the path; his feet knew where they were going. He carried a paper bag with two pumpkin muffins. Sandy wanted him to have breakfast tomorrow morning. He smiled. Even with no sign of Hollywood, he was still a performer. He still liked entertaining a crowd. Was this the spark he carried into this life? With nothing else to his name, it came to him naturally, it seemed to be what he had to offer. And it made him happy. Also, it was better than cleaning off pumpkins.

PART 7

His chattering teeth woke him. The center of the dark windshield glowed and flickered. Sylvan moved the blanket off his face and breathed out a cold cloud. The Chevette was freezing but it looked like there was a fire outside. His teeth were going like Morse code. If it really was a fire—if it wasn't that bird returned—he could get warm.

He sat up. He couldn't see much out the icy windshield, but something was burning on the ground in front of the car. His fingers were numb, his hands thumped like mittens on the door latch. Wedging his wooden fingers under the latch, he managed to pull it, then he had to lean into the door and push. It popped free of its frozen seal and Sylvan staggered out. He didn't know if it was the middle of the night or nearly morning. Not more than six feet in front of the car, just before the tidal wave of blackberries began, a campfire had been placed. Round river stones circled it. It drew Sylvan right to it. The heat poured into him.

Any questions about how it came to be here were sighed away. Oh, it felt so good to be warm.

Sylvan opened his eyes and stared at the fire. For a minute, he wondered if he might be in a dream. The flames were coming from the broken pumpkin he put in that spot hours ago when he cleaned out his car. The fire just steadily burned away, throwing off light and heat.

Earlier, before he went to Clouds, he didn't know what to do with the pumpkin. Knowing it was worth something, he didn't want to throw it in the leaves. Now he was glad he didn't. He could have burned down all the blackberries. And what if he left it in his car when he went to sleep! Sylvan held out his hands to its heat. The pumpkin burned slowly, the edges seemed to melt in the air.

He sat next to the ring of stones someone laid down. Was there someone watching out for him? It felt so very good to be warm and Sylvan let himself slide down. The grass was soft. The pumpkin fire crackled pleasantly. It was so easy to fall back asleep.

George served him a hot bowl of oatmeal and said, "This is from Sandy. She left me a note in the kitchen, told me to make you this." There were sliced strawberries on top.

"Thank you." Sylvan put his coffee cup on the table next to it. Even the coffee was pumpkin flavored, but of course he had grown accustomed to that taste in everything.

"I didn't know you told stories," George said. "Sounds like people liked it."

Sylvan shrugged and smiled. "I have a lot more. There's so much I've learned since then." He felt good and not just because of the hot food and kindness he was shown. You would have thought sleeping on the ground in the winter would wear you out, but Sylvan felt good, as if that pumpkin fire had actually been a sort of medicine.

Back in the kitchen, the big pot boiling on the stove overflowed and hissed. George turned from the table. "Next time," he said, "I'll be here to listen." He called over his shoulder from the stove, "You going to be here tonight?"

"I hope so."

"Alright then." George's voice was part of the cooking now, the chopping, boiling, the radio song.

Sylvan spooned at a strawberry. He knew what they tasted like back in his old world. He wondered if this one would taste like pumpkin.

The studio audience cheered for The Knick Knacks. Their song "South of Peoria" still hung in the air, the pretty guitar riff and the brushing cymbal, floating over stage, fading.

Sylvan Moore carried his microphone out towards them. "Ladies and gentlemen," he said, "The Knick Knacks." Sylvan shook the guitarist's hand and patted the drummer on the arm. "Weren't they something?" he asked as the applause began to calm. "Thank you, boys."

The red QUIET light flashed above the tier of chairs. A technician off camera held his finger to his lips. Sylvan wanted to speak again.

"How long you been at this?"

The guitarist leaned towards the microphone, "This year makes fifty."

"Is that right?"

"Yes sir."

"And how old are you, if you don't mind my asking?"

"I'm sixty five."

"Sixty five!" Sylvan turned to face the audience. "And how about your partner there, behind the drum kit?"

"Dale is 67."

Sylvan shook his head in amazement. "And the two of you have been playing your music for fifty years?"

"Yes sir."

"In bars, on street corners?"

"Wherever they will have us."

"You and Dale persisted all this time?" Sylvan clucked.

"That's correct."

"Never got to quit your day jobs, or go in a big recording studio?"

"No, Dale and I—"

Sylvan continued, "Never got to see your name on the marquee or the big city papers. No tour bus, no fans, no record deals, cars or mansions?"

Another flashing light went on over the audience and they all groaned as one wave that swept across The Knick Knacks.

Sylvan Moore held up his hand, "And yet tonight, after fifty years of playing to a *desert,* you land here on the stage of *Winners & Losers,* to perform before a TV audience of millions."

Sylvan stepped back to allow the big camera to close in and frame the two old men. "The Knick Knacks!" Sylvan said, and as he raised his arm, everyone in the tiers of chairs joined him in asking, "Winners or Losers?"

Sylvan sat by the river for a while. It was cold but the sunshine felt good. He found a wooden chair by a dumpster and dragged it to this spot. He liked watching the water. The river was alive and always going somewhere. A funny thought appeared. What if he was presented on *Winners & Losers* right now? Looking like he rolled down the river in his shabby clothes, the audience couldn't help but gasp at the state of Sylvan Moore. He would seem like a loser at the end of his rope and they would all be ready to vote based on that. But then he would take the microphone from the new shiny host and he would tell everyone what he found out.

Wouldn't that be something?

He did have that thought before and he did think about what he would say into all those millions of TV sets. There were plenty of times in cold nights and hiding out of the rain when he worked those words through his head. Wasn't he ready to try? Didn't they need to know? The only problem was, it meant going back.

In just these weeks he lived in town, he probably knew it better than people who grew up here. He knew more than the stores and the stoplights. Sylvan lived on the streets, he knew where to go in what kind of weather (how the wind blew on Harris and where to hide from the rain) and above all the best place for sunshine. He could trace his hand along a brick wall in the dark and know where to walk. He uncovered the town like no map ever could.

When you live this way you start to tune in to the world. You become part of the world in a way you weren't before.

After watching the river for an hour or so, Sylvan left the chair with the broken arm rest and walked upstream a little bit. Past the docks where he worked yesterday, he followed a scrabbled path under the pier with the Lighthouse restaurant above and the slats let daylight fall in stripes on the mud between the pilings. He had been through here on nights when there was no light. The path picked up after those shadows and climbed the bank again, among the weeds and the ribs of a long dead pumpkin boat.

Parking lots, fenced-in yards, the backs of buildings and now and again a tree. This was upstream from where his car was hidden. It wasn't quite out of town but it was close. It wasn't to the pumpkin fields, but you could see them in the distance. Sylvan felt at home. Sometimes the path led him right next to the river. He saw some of his old footprints filled with water. It made him look forward to summer. He could imagine the warm sun, the dry grass underfoot. There were birds singing on the wires, swallows, blue sky everywhere. He was going to find a nice spot and lay on his back and watch the clouds.

The other morning he found a puddle skimmed with a thin layer of ice. Summer was a wish in the future.

The river had a gray look to it today. It was

just the way. As the path climbed, the fields came into view, an orange smudge behind a line of poplar trees.

Sylvan also spotted the fish ladder just ahead.

Made of clear plastic steps, it rose from the water and then ran over land in a long trough you could walk under before it dropped and fed back into the river.

It was like some magical stream that made a channel in the air. Salmon caught in the sunlight gleamed like new silver cars on an assembly line. They were in the sky and given a chance to see the place they were traveling through—the woods and mountains, farms and fields. And you could walk up close to the plastic and make eye contact with those fish as they slowly wagged by. Where had they been, what had they seen on the long journey out to sea and finally back to where they started?

Sylvan walked along with one, from the steps, watched it splash into the trough and soar across to the next set of steps. It went over the waterfalls and Sylvan kept his eye on that one as it moved in the foaming current, until it rested in a tank at Sylvan's eyelevel. The fish gave him a good long look too. Jaw moving up and down like someone talking, it reminded Sylvan of the deer he saw just before that forest stream flooded. Another salmon pushed it along, and with a flick of its tail the fish was gone. The ladder splashed back in the river. There was still a long way for that fish to go.

PART 8

When something is gone that's supposed to be there, its absence is almost physical, like a big block of cold outer space. The blackberries were there, the boat was there, the path with dandelions had not disappeared…but the little blue Chevette was gone. A yellow line of tape was strung across that cove where it had been. NO TRESPASSING was repeated in black letters like Morse code along it.

Sylvan ducked beneath the tape and stared at the pale crushed square in the weeds where his car had stood. His first thought was: There goes everything. What would he do now? Where would he go? Why did this have to happen?

Someone walked around from behind the boat. They made a crackling sort of sound like newspapers rolled across the weeds. Sylvan was slow to notice—he was thinking of where his life was now…he was thinking emptiness.

"They come and took your car."

The afternoon winter light played with shadows and it did make it hard to see the man's face. Sylvan recognized those clothes though—the straw hat, and the lanky almost weightless way the figure leaned against the bow like a bundle of twisted straw.

Without too much surprise, Sylvan realized it was the scarecrow he gave a ride to the first day he drove into town.

"Tough luck," the scarecrow said.

Sylvan agreed, "Yes."

The scarecrow rustled scratchily closer to Sylvan. "They probly don't like you setting fires."

Sylvan looked to where the pumpkin had burnt a black circle on the grass.

"That was me done that," the scarecrow admitted with a shrug. "Gets cold this time a year."

"Yes," Sylvan said. "It will get a lot colder once that sun goes down. I need to find somewhere to go for the night."

"Don't worry. I know a place." The scarecrow walked past Sylvan, "Follow me."

By the time they reached the field outside of town, daylight was gone. Sylvan stared up at the moon. At least the car thieves hadn't taken that, the only source of light.

"Mind the vines," the scarecrow warned Sylvan. The field was tangled with a network of vines, crisscrossing between the pumpkins.

Finally Sylvan had to ask, "Are we sleeping in the middle of this field?"

"That's right."

"Well… There's a good chance I might freeze to death."

The scarecrow laughed. "I keep telling you, don't worry. Look, see that?"

Ahead of them, Sylvan spotted something in the gloom. It looked like a rabbit hutch raised above the field on spindly legs.

"Beehive," the scarecrow explained.

Fine, Sylvan thought, I'll sleep in a beehive. I'm so tired I could sleep in a can of beans.

The scarecrow really knew his way around the field, moving light-footed as a waltzer while Sylvan tripped on pumpkin vines.

"Careful," the scarecrow would hiss every time.

Sylvan kept his hands balled inside his coat sleeves, but his face felt icy cold, lips numb, still it was better to be moving. The thought of sleeping in his car was now a luxury. Sometimes he looked out across the field washed in silver moonlight, mostly he had to keep his eyes on the ground. They must have been in the very center of the crop. The plaid shirt of the scarecrow shook like a sail as he held up his arm. "Made it," he whispered hoarsely.

"The beehive," Sylvan whispered back. His mouth was too cold to ask why they were whispering.

"You make yourself at home."

Sylvan crept around the scarecrow and stared at the beehive door. It was no bigger than a barrel. "Do I have to get inside of it?"

The scarecrow stifled a laugh with his ratty glove. "Not unless you want to get stung to death." He shook his head, making sure he heard that all right so he could retell it later tomorrow in some field with other scarecrows. "No, those bees wouldn't like waking up in the middle of a winter night. You just take your coat off for a pillow and lie underneath on the earth."

"Take my coat off?"

"You'll be plenty warm."

Sylvan didn't know what to say.

"Trust me."

Sylvan walked on the frozen clods of soil until he got close to the beehive. He held his hand out to it.

"Underneath is where it's warm," the scarecrow hissed.

The beehive was set up on four pine legs and there was plenty of room for him to crawl under there. "Okay…" Sylvan whispered. "Why not?"

It was true though. When Sylvan got low enough to feel the air below, it was as if the beehive was blowing down heat. The ground was soft as a blanket.

"Pleasant dreams," said the scarecrow.

"Okay…" It felt strange to do, but Sylvan took off his coat and folded it up for a pillow. He got under the beehive and curled up. The warmth felt so good he didn't care how it was happening. His eyes closed and all at once he was gone.

Sylvan Moore never slept below a beehive before. There's no sleep like it. The heat that radiated and the slumbering hum of those hundred dreaming bees led him floating as far from the world as an astronaut.

He could have stayed out there, it would have been okay adrift in a million stars, but he returned to the planet. Daylight opened his eyes.

He stretched. As his feet pressed out beyond the umbrella of the beehive, he felt cool air on his ankles. He pulled his legs up and rolled onto his back and blinked. Morning under a beehive.

"About time you woke up."

Sylvan turned his head and saw the scarecrow.

"You sleep good?"

Sylvan rubbed his eyes. "I could have kept sleeping forever."

The scarecrow barked with laughter. The leaves on the vines rippled like a rushing stream. "You hungry?"

Now that he mentioned it, Sylvan was.

"Have some honey. That hive can't hold it all."

The scarecrow was right. There was a seam

where some honey burbled out. Sylvan swept it with two fingers and tasted it.

"Good?" The scarecrow laughed again. "I knew you'd like it." He had a laugh like a crow. Sylvan also realized this was the best he felt in a long time, probably since the California coast.

"That's all you need though," the scarecrow held up a cautioning hand. "Just that taste keep you strong all day."

Sylvan really wanted another taste of that honey. The scarecrow was right though—Sylvan felt wide awake now, stocked like a roaring wood stove. He popped out from under the beehive.

He picked up his coat and put it on. It was a chilly morning in the middle of a pumpkin field. He could see his breath.

"You ever try scarecrowing?"

"No. I was in television."

"Yeah, I know. *Winners & Losers*. I seen it."

"Really?" Sylvan was shocked.

"I got my own TV. I watch it when the crows go to sleep."

"I didn't think my program aired this far. Nobody seems to have watched it. Just you."

"I didn't say I watched it. I seen it when I turned channels."

"Oh."

The breeze seemed to sigh through the leaves around them.

The scarecrow's face, painted on burlap cloth, showed concern by wrinkling up, "What I want to know is would you mind taking over my job for a spell?"

"You want me to be a scarecrow?" Sylvan shrugged, "If it will help, sure."

The scarecrow clapped his gloves together and hollered, "You hear that? He said yes!"

The crop trembled around them, stirring and murmuring. If he would have known, Sylvan would have leaped atop the beehive and flown it back to town. He never had the chance. The ground was slithering with vines. Quick as pouring water they wrapped around his ankles and held Sylvan tight.

"Thanks pal," the scarecrow said. "I'll show you your work station." The scarecrow didn't have any trouble with vines underfoot.

Sylvan lifted a leg to follow and felt the hold on him release. They allowed him to walk along behind the scarecrow. He had a feeling they would seize him again if he tried running away.

"There." The scarecrow pointed at a wooden platform ten feet above the field. A ladder went up a pole to a perched rocking chair.

Sylvan asked, "What do I do?"

"You watch for crows."

Sylvan saw a break of blue showing in the gray cloud cover, but he didn't see any crows. "What do I do if I see a crow?"

They were nearly there. The dirt path took them to it.

"I'll tell you all that," the scarecrow said. He reached the ladder and bounded up. Sylvan wasn't so sure though. The structure looked only made for someone filled with straw.

Sylvan put his foot on the bottom rung and tested his weight. The pole creaked. The platform swayed. The rungs seemed brittle as the bones of some skeleton. Sylvan took a breath, holding the air like a balloon and climbed it in a hurry.

The scarecrow reached his plaid covered arm down and pulled Sylvan up to the shaky platform. "Whoa! Never been more than me up here before. Careful!" The scarecrow grabbed Sylvan's coat. "Don't fall!"

"I'm okay. Thanks."

With a groan, the platform steadied.

"It's a little scary," Sylvan admitted. "What a view though. You can see the whole valley, the farms, the river, the town."

The scarecrow scratched the back of his neck and left a straw standing up. "Well, I'm glad you like it. I had my fill." His button eyes started towards the river, "Crows be on the way soon."

Sylvan looked for them. Except for that touch of blue, the sky was a cloudy gray pond. "How long do I need to be a scarecrow?" he asked.

"Not so long as me I hope," the scarecrow said.

"I mean, for an hour? Until this afternoon? I can't be out here all day though, I have to go find my car."

The scarecrow scratched his neck again, found that troublesome stem of hay and pulled it free. He flicked it off the edge of the platform. There were hundreds of pumpkins growing around them.

"Oh!" Sylvan could see two black specks leaving an oak tree at the corner of the field. "Crows!"

The scarecrow swiveled and looked.

"What do I do?" Sylvan asked.

"Nothing. Them aren't crows."

"They look like crows."

"Crows come by river. Look! See them?"

Sylvan could hear them too. The high metallic whine of the outboard motors carried across the field, cutting the air like a saw. Sylvan counted five boats coming from town, the same boats he saw leave from the docks in the morning, the same ones he helped unload. They slowed and stopped against the shore, the cattails and the willow. Just up the gulley bank lay a thousand pumpkins in the field.

"Grab the horn!" the scarecrow ordered. "It's on the chair."

The platform shifted as Sylvan rushed to get the megaphone off the rocking chair. He noticed a small black TV set on the floorboards. "What do I do with this?"

"Holler!" the scarecrow said. "Start hollering!"

Sylvan neared the edge of the platform, could feel it buckle a little. Across the field, people were leaving their boats. Sylvan lifted the megaphone and said, "Hey!" He was surprised how loud his voice flew out.

"That's right," the scarecrow said. He had his feet on the ladder.

"Are you leaving?"

"It's your job now," the scarecrow sunk a

step, "You're my replacement."

"Wait a minute…"

"Keep hollering! You need to scare them!" The scarecrow waved a ragged glove, "Good luck," and sunk from sight.

Sylvan turned around. The people were edging into the field. Sylvan saw a pumpkin yanked from the ground.

"Hey!" he yelled again. "Stop doing that!"

PART 9

At the end of the day one thing was certain: Sylvan Moore was not a good scarecrow. Some of the people even waved to him as they carried pumpkins away. Maybe he just didn't know what to say. It wasn't his audience. He bombed. Oh, he felt badly for the crop. Those people walked right in and took what they wanted. They got quite a lot before they got back in the boats and left. His words were only wind.

Sylvan leaned back in the rocking chair and stared at the moon. Half of it was gone too.

He was thankful for whoever left him the electric blanket. They also left a pumpkin with two outlet holes bored into its shell. One for the blanket and one, he supposed, for the TV. With the blanket plugged in, he was warm, staring up at the nighttime sky.

Of all the things, his thoughts brought him way back. He grew up in farmland not so different than this. He remembered walking to school talent show one night in the pouring rain.

He didn't even mind.

He was soaked.

The weather didn't matter though. All that

rain was only washing him. He walked along the rills of the plowed field until he got to the road. Then it was only another mile to town.

He was lucky. A truck slowed down and waited for him on the shoulder ahead.

Sylvan ran to it and opened the passenger door.

The driver turned down the radio. She said, "What are you doing out in the rain?"

He jumped in the car and soon he told her how much he liked the girl at school. He didn't even know who was driving him there, but he told her everything. It seemed like the most important thing in the world. And she drove like an ambulance, going through yellow traffic lights, taking corners at 30 MPH. When they got there, Sylvan jumped back out into the rain and the driver told him, "Good luck!"

It was a black sky held over him and he was wet again. He didn't mind. He was getting closer to her.

He closed the door and ran in the rain. Every day the school bus let him off in this spot. He ran under the sheltered aisle that led to the gymnasium. He felt like a fish.

Those people around the door stepped aside as he entered.

What a golden bright light. The gym was a wax lantern and he quickly found a seat on the bleachers.

He saw the end of Ian and the Ions. The drums crashed out of a garbage can, pouring with a cloud of dry ice. The crowd on the steps loved it and stomped and clapped as Sylvan looked for her. The rest of the performers were lined along the wall, under the scoreboard. Where was she?

Everyone was clapping. Sylvan put his hands together too.

Sylvan was just in time. Her name floated out of the speakers and he watched her walk to the microphone.

He was so in love with her, soaked like he fell in a lake, and she was a candle in that white dress with her long brown hair.

At that time he didn't know all the courage it took her to sing with only the piano. Oh, how he wished he knew then what he knew now. What was the use of a memory if you wished you could act differently?

He listened to her, felt every word sent to him and when she was done he clapped like everyone.

Whatever happened to her? How was he

supposed to know?

The thought of her left him and he was alone in the rocking chair. No, he wasn't alone, there were as many thoughts as there were pumpkins out in the crop. He couldn't help but bump into another one. He just didn't want to.

The TV was sitting right at his feet. All he had to do was plug it into the pumpkin and something would carry him off to sleep. "Tonight on *Winners & Losers*, a scarecrow who can't scare." Sylvan smiled and told the night, "I wanted to talk about the meaning of life and instead I'm stuck doing this pointless job."

How long was he supposed to try? Another day, a week, a month, a season? Was the scarecrow ever going to come back to relieve him?

He rocked and looked at the sky. The moon was only a pale glow behind the clouds. His breath steamed out to join them. Sylvan shut his eyes. He needed to rest. There would be a lot of yelling tomorrow.

PART 10

The next day was the same as the day before, as was the rest of the week. On Friday the boats were pulled up on the bank and the people were a lot closer. Sylvan didn't need the megaphone. He paced back and forth on the platform waving his arms, reciting Shakespeare. But not even Othello would scare off the crows. He tried all the speeches he could remember. He threw himself back into the role of producer, shouting orders at the crew and poor Artie and Chives. None of his rants made a difference. The crows took what they wanted.

"Sylvan?"

The platform stopped shaking and he brought his arms down.

"Is this where you've been hiding?"

Sylvan remembered the man. It was Jimmy. He was holding pumpkins. They were the last ones in the field. The crop had been cleared.

Finally quiet, Sylvan stared around him at the trampled ground. How could the crows have been so greedy? It was all gone.

"Can you leave one?" Sylvan croaked.

"What?"

His voice was raw as sandpaper, he couldn't

speak anymore.

Someone called from the boats and the crow said, "Well, I guess we'll see you around."

Sylvan held to the rail, spindly as a willow branch, and watched the last pumpkins go. The field looked like a prairie with no more buffalo.

The boat motors started. Low in the water, the flock of them backed out into the river and flew for town.

They carried the sound of the pumpkins with them too. Sylvan had grown so used to the sound of the leaves scratching, or patting the orange bellies laying in rows.

There was nothing tying Sylvan to this place anymore.

He crossed the tipping platform to the ladder side and saw someone waiting for him on the ground below. He guessed the painted eyes weren't happy with him. "I'm sorry," Sylvan rasped.

"What for?" the scarecrow asked.

"I didn't do a good job as a scarecrow," Sylvan wanted to say. He couldn't though. His voice was rusted shut.

"C'mon down!" the scarecrow called. "Bring that pumpkin with you."

Sylvan turned back to the rocking chair and

unplugged the cord from the blanket. He never did need to connect the TV. He liked the sky. He would miss sitting in the chair, watching the nighttime come on. He carried the warm pumpkin back to the ladder.

"Careful!" the scarecrow warned, "That's the last one."

As he walked away from the field, Sylvan thought about that last pumpkin. After they buried it, covered it with dirt and patted the ground, the scarecrow said it wouldn't be long. He watered the spot and told Sylvan the good news. He could go.

Sylvan kept his hands warm in his coat pockets, pushed in straw. All his pockets were filled with straw. The scarecrow had even lined his coat and stuffed some in his shoes. It worked too. Sylvan was warm. And he was free again, puffing breath in the cold air like a steam engine with the whole world before him. What a feeling!

He picked up a stone and threw it far ahead of him. He couldn't see where it landed, somewhere halfway to the river, halfway to the mountains beyond.

MOUNTAIN TEMPLE

THE 1861 LETTER

After I finished the *Homeless Sutra* adventure, I wasn't sure what to write next. I was reading a lot of Japan: *The Zen Teaching of Homeless Kodo*, Ryokan, Soun Nakagawa, Hosai Ozaki, *Zen Flesh Zen Bones*. Waiting in between writing is a strange cloudy world. Then *Mountain Temple* floated into sight.

Just before that happened though, I dreamed of a letter. It was sunny and I read it in the tree shade by a river. I recognized the handwriting. The letter was from a friend I knew, telling me he was alive again in 1861. He got thrown back there when he died.

Can dreams be used to send messages? Do they show us travel through time? If so, the letter didn't let me read it too closely; the words were like moving water.

That was alright though. I understood. Dreams leave you with a feeling. When I woke up, I went downstairs and made tea and coffee. I like that hour before I leave. That's when this book began.

Although there is in heaven and earth a something infinitely quick of hearing and infinitely sharp of sight, independent of conditions of time or space, present as if actually on the spot, passing to and fro without any interval, embodying itself in all things which are, and filling the universe, it has neither form nor voice, and is therefore not cognizable by our senses.

—The Cloud-Men of Yamato

Look at the sky. There's another world happening. If you look carefully you may see me.

In the hold where the poetry is written, benches are set with candles and pots of steaming tea.

One little window of yellow light is looking out.

This story begins when they took me from my spot and chose me to navigate. Everyone gets a chance to fly the cloud temple.

How do you steer the temple to its next destination? All the poems keep us aloft and our thoughts direct us. Imagine a place and we're there.

The first time, I took us to a moonlit field. I knew where to go. When I opened the door, I went down the steps, into the tall weeds and wildflowers where I found a pool of water. They swam right up to me as if waiting.

We caught them in a glass bowl and took them with us.

Two orange goldfish suspended like candlelight in the dark water.

I knew who to bring them to. I already wrote a poem about it. It was waiting to come true.

There was more to my plan than goldfish, but it would have to happen the next time I flew.

We ride the tide in the sky, hidden by clouds, and we can slip just as easily through time.

For my next turn, they brought me a lantern and a stack of paper scraps. I knew what they were—the poetry written down below. We drop the poems into the furnace to keep the temple flying.

It was always a dream of mine and soon we hovered above the rooftops of old Baltimore, coal smoke, cold black night.

I carefully stepped from the temple grounds onto the steep tiles, where I climbed the roof outside the window of Edgar Allan Poe.

I left the goldfish for him to find. Curtains covered only half the window.

I like to create minor miracles, it's not like I'm making it rain frogs. Everyone in the temple has their own way.

We can't communicate with the world in words. If you heard us, it would just sound like rain or poured sand.

I don't mean to sound mysterious. We would just be lost in the static, a whisper on a faraway radio station.

That's the one memory I have of my life before the temple—listening to the radio—but what was I listening for?

Some days are nice up here. Dragonflies appear in the sunshine. The temple hums like a beehive.

We float along like the tip of a mountain, a hill with a temple, surrounded by a garden and a pine tree, dew on the bristles.

The hillside is terraced for growing tea. A network of bamboo channels water for the temple. Once I found a stream had broken free. It ran from a broken gutter to where it poured off the garden edge to the land below.

In the kitchen is a rack full of bottled clouds, many different kinds to suit our need. I chose a snowy colored one and poured it out the little window. The cloud will wrap itself around and keep us from being seen.

Our existence is a secret. We have to remain hidden.

I don't know much about the lives below. Sometimes I catch a glimpse of them before we hide ourselves again.

When I watch them from the telescope, I see them drive cars, go to schools or jobs. Otherwise they're just wandering around. I guess I look for someone like me looking back.

We're not alone in the sky. Yesterday we found ourselves in the same flight path as a flock of snow geese.

There's always the chance of seeing another temple too. When you're floating along, you never know.

It happened once. We sailed alongside each other with all the prayer flags rattling in the wind.

Looking out the window, nothing but white.

There was nothing to see in the air until I heard a crow somewhere.

It's been a while since we touched land and I'm pleased it's my turn again.

With a plush sigh, we landed in the snow. The trees wore white coats.

It's as comforting and calm as the land of sleep.

Under the branches I heard the sound of the melting drops landing in the snow.

I could also see bird and animal tracks.

Crackle and bend of the cold leaves, my foot-steps.

The light on the snow made me think of the moon.

Would the moon be interesting to visit? It's a long ocean voyage in the night to a colder world than here.

We're in a winter climate. I like it, but I also wish we were somewhere warm.

As soon as I get back to the temple, I will write a poem about Fiji. That's part of my plan.

I meant to grab the first handful of snow and return but I didn't. That would have changed my future, but I wandered further.

All this work for setting goldfish on a window sill? Or keeping a snowball frozen until we get to the South Seas? Yes, it will be worth it. It's another miracle someone will never forget. They will wonder how something like that could happen. One small event will amaze them.

I could see myself in Fiji, the snowball turning wet. I would have to find someplace to put it fast. While I bent down to cup the snow, I heard the bell on the hill.

Someone was calling me back to the temple.

I had to be careful walking, don't slip, the snow can be treacherous.

When I passed a winter tree, the remaining leaves hissed at me.

The fog whirled about the hill like the stripes on a top. There was no sign of the temple on top. They left me.

I arrived back there too late. There was a shape pressed deep in the field where the temple had been. Now it was somewhere in the clouds and I was left stuck on the ground.

The air swirled white.

Snowflakes seem to like falling through space. There's a chirp, a chickadee I'm guessing, up in the tree.

Oh, I thought, maybe I understand what happened. They left me here on purpose. People in the temple come and go. You never know when someone will leave to make room for someone new.

This must be what happens when we disappear. Really it's the flying temple leaving us.

I can move quiet as an animal. I walked right past a deer. A fox turned and watched me. The birds carried on as usual.

My feet were starting to get cold. I said something that should have warmed them, but my poetry doesn't work here.

A deer path led downhill, toward a road probably, toward a town somewhere.

I could picture myself two years from now. Marooned. I'm living in a city, walking under monorails, rain off of awnings.

I rent a room on top of an apartment building. In the summer people dry their clothes on lines strung overhead like clipper sails.

I live on the roof, in an old shed that used to belong to pigeons.

Every day, pigeons return. I guess a memory drives them here, the same as me.

I try to read their minds, but who knows what a pigeon is thinking? They nest all night on the roof while I write. Still, I keep hoping to hear from the temple.

I buy a radio and every night I tune across the dial looking for their signal.

That's why I took this spot on the roof. I'm closer to the sky.

I'm a telescope. I see moths and crows and airplanes.

I watch an eagle. It is a sliver in the city smog. I lose it among all the lines of electric wires.

Even in a city, the sky is so big. Imagine finding the little speck of the temple floating in the air.

That future possibility seemed so real I had to stop myself and remind myself where I was: here, on a snowy path, and what happens will be a mystery.

I was no longer part of the sky. Across the bay from me I could see the row of mountains touched by sun.

The snowy top of a mountain on the horizon looked so far away, but I wondered if the temple was there.

I was always sure there were people on earth who were aware of the mountain temple and now I am one of them.

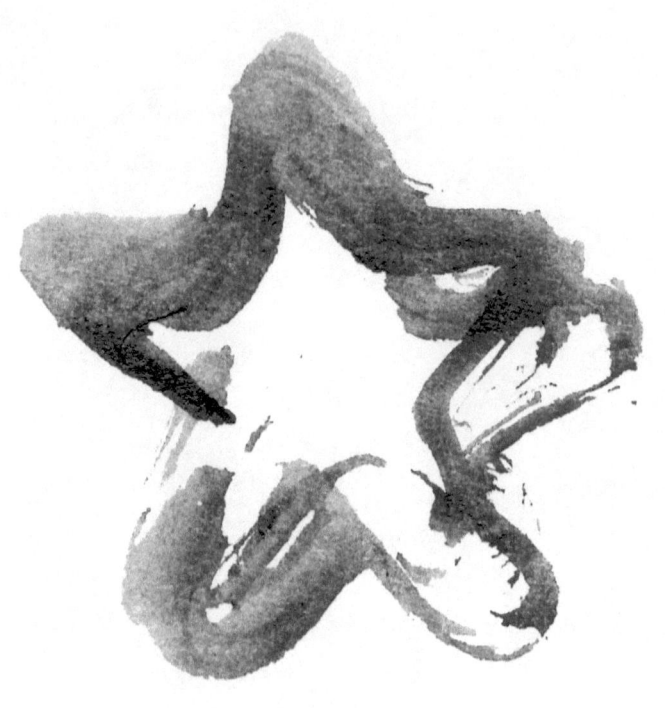

INSTANT CROW

3 SENTENCE APOLOGY

I tried to make *Instant Crow* a comedy. This was supposed to be a funny world where every little thing was for sale. Instead, it became Groucho Marx meets Karl Marx in the rain.

I can't believe they sent me here. All it does is rain in this town, day after day, night after night, and months pass and I'm peddling the last thing anyone wants: water.

Anyway, that's my job. I have to make the best of it. And you know what? Part of me believes this is just a test. If I do good, maybe something better will happen next.

I didn't have much time to think about that before I ran into a ghost.

Their world exists in the same space as ours, like a shadow laid on top.

She came out of the wall and for a moment I thought she will pass through me like a glass of cold water.

That didn't happen though. She was real alright and all that white burst like a cloud.

She had form and substance and a sound like a church bell when I ran into her.

Some of her color stayed on me, my coat and leg where we collided.

I said, "I'm sorry! I thought you were a ghost." But now I could see she was just painted to look that way.

"I sell flour." She carried it in a suitcase like mine. There were people watching us from the bakery.

The rain sounded like a coin-operated thing rattling and ringing down the spout.

We both had places to be. The fine rain was already washing our meeting away.

Wasn't it a sort of comedy? I should have known from her dress—a ghost doesn't wear polk-a-dots.

The street was crowded with people hustling. You name it, you'll see it being sold. I'm no different, I suppose. I carry a big sample book filled with every kind of water you could want.

I could go door to door. People do. Every door is a flower you can stop and buzz about, but I'm not that sort of bumbling bee. I go where I know I'm needed.

For instance, the Botanical Gardens. It sits like a prism on top of the distant hill with its glassy walls twinkling. They would be happy to see me. After all, where else can they get 20 feet of Amazon, or the mist off Machu Picchu? That kind of stuff doesn't just fall from the sky.

Yes, this sample book I lug around has page after page of wonders. If you're in the market for water, I've got puddles, streams, rivers, ponds, lakes, and even a sea nobody has seen for years.

I don't mean to sound pushy but we all have to make a living. Actually, truth be told, I can't wait for the day when I won't have to sell anymore. I imagine that old me, in a little tin trailer, far away on the bank of a free running stream.

But retirement is years away. I've got to make hay while the sun shines (or rake seaweed while it rains). Like all the rest of us, I got in line on the sidewalk to wait for the next city bus.

"Umbrellas! Who wants an umbrella? You don't have to stand and get wet. I've got umbrellas for every budget." Oh, the minute you stop moving you become a target.

"Hey fellah! You going somewhere important? You don't want to be late! My watches are guaranteed to always get you there in time." I averted my eyes and watched the street. The wheels go rushing by.

Three pedal cars stopped, the drivers leaned out their plastic windows to haggle price, and two of the people waiting in line left with them. At the last second before the bus arrived, someone else jumped on a milk truck running board.

I paid the fare and was lucky enough to get a seat in back. The old man next to me had not paid the window though. It remained tightly shut. There was nothing to look at but the metal curtain.

Outside didn't matter to him. He was reading a library book. He needed a pocketful of coins to turn the pages. I watched him put a nickel in the binding and then he gave me a glare. He thought I was reading for free over his shoulder.

So I stared straight ahead, down the aisle. The windshield steamed like a television screen, all gray with a movie shot on the run.

How much longer am I here anyway? Until I finish my quota. I could stretch out my hand and touch that number. For now it's just out of reach.

When you're in a town where it always rains, you need to sell a different kind of water. Yesterday I installed a Japanese hot spring in a backyard. Will someone in Hokkaido notice their pool is gone?

One time I almost bought a rundown wishing well. I was in some small town on my travels and I found it beside a parking lot. It must have been there for years…maybe before there were cars. Did it remember horses and the shade from tall trees? Was it using all its sad coin power to wish itself back?

When the bus stopped, I carried my book down the aisle, out the door to the sidewalk. I was confident and the rain carried me and whispered that I was on the way.

Everything is built on a slant. If you took these houses and set them on flat ground, they would be leaning crazily, bent in a speedy rush to be somewhere else.

Across the next street, the park looked soggy and green as eelgrass.

Some people gathered below a tree. They're still trying to get the animals to pay like we do. The squirrels seem willing, interested in offered crumbs, but they don't have pockets or wallets.

You can either go through the park on a path that winds like a long loop of silk across the lawn, or you can climb the steep wooden stairway that leads straight to the Botanical Gardens.

Halfway to the top I stopped. The wood was shiny wet and I put my hand on the damp rail and turned. The town below had become miniature, dark trees grown among gray roads, while chimneys steamed in the rain.

For only a few dollars from someone, I could open my book and pick out a waterfall. I could lean over the railing and place it among the fiddleheads. This could be the first note of an orchestra.

When I got to the top I was tired and I almost bought a calm breath from the woman selling them there. She held them clutched like balloons.

It was nearly quiet. But a man was selling birdsongs. You could wear one on your coat like a flower.

The real birds were on the glass roof of the building. They could see lemon trees below them. They could feel the heat of that world in there. They were saving their songs for that day.

Next to the door was a sign: THE BOTANICAL GARDENS. NO PEDDLERS. A lot of places say that. But I didn't come all this way, carrying I don't know how many gallons, to be turned away by words.

I went inside and right away they knew I was there to sell. A guard caught me before I even got to the ticket booth. "Wait!" I said, "Allow me to explain."

"You may not realize it, but all these plants have feeling and memories, instinctive likes and dislikes. If you're feeding them ordinary water, how can you expect them to be extraordinary?"

"Allow me," I tried again, backed up into the corner by the door. A potted plant stood there, a sunflower waiting to be brushed by the drops off a Kansas rainbow.

I have just the water for it, only in my haste, with the guard pulling my sleeve, I gave it Polar Sleet instead…These samples really need to be better organized.

The flower shivered and drooped and I was thrown right out the door.

I have made mistakes before. Once someone was thirsty and I gave them a glass of dishwater.

Why do I even have that sample in my book? I don't know. I scooped it from a kitchen café sink for the lonely story it told.

Loneliness doesn't mean you haven't lived. My book is filled with places I have been. Still, I'd rather share them with someone else.

Once I sold a wave to a girl. That was a long time ago and I'm not proud of the memory. I told her it was rare and it would be with her forever and it would follow wherever she went.

What about the wind? I haven't mentioned it much. Does it push against you when you're out in the rain? Well not so much in this town. It stays pretty still. The rain is all the weather we need.

I was getting wet again. I looked up at the sky and could see each drop of rain had a life of its own, rushing at the ground like traffic.

I must have looked a little lost staring up at the sky. It didn't take long before they were trying to sell me maps, a pocket guide to birds, and an astronomy chart.

There are people who chase after the sale, who make that the sole purpose of their life. Mostly I'm worried about that sunflower—I hope it will be okay.

I started down the stairs and noticed something I didn't see before: a mossy chair, all crooked in the blackberries, caught like a horse riding up hill.

All the things people bought they don't want any more end up adding layers to the earth. That's one good thing about my water. It just washes away.

I passed the spot where I wanted to start a waterfall. Not today, maybe some other time. But I did wonder: Did I come all this way for nothing?

Last week I was getting desperate for a little cash, enough for the rent that was due, so I stood on the curb and sold carwashes. Yes, I have a page for that. Nobody was looking in Nebraska when I took $50 worth of steam and soapy water.

It's not easy to make a living this way. I've been collecting water for years.

What I really wish I was selling is good dreams. That's something everybody wants. It seems like that's half my competition out there. If only I had a book full of those. I could have been selling other worlds.

There's someone in my apartment who owns the first week of spring, when the cherry trees start to bloom. I hardly ever see him leave his room.

I was watching my shoes walk me down, lost in future possibilities when suddenly all the wet driftwood of those stairs ran into land.

Yes, this is what all those steamship passengers felt after days on the ocean. The ground is still, but you carry a phantom motion.

Has anyone ever counted those steps? I wasn't about to but I'd like to know. There's always someone you can pay to do what you don't want to do.

How many steps *had* it been? I was just curious. Maybe they could put that on a sign? 354 stairs from here to there.

I decided to walk. The cost of bus fare was something I could turn into a small meal later on.

I thought of that sunflower. I didn't mean what happened…and I remember saying sorry as they tossed me out. I was just trying to help.

Block by block that sunflower became a villain in my mind. I wondered if it had planned this all along. It occurred to me that it might have been smirking as it held its petals doubled over.

What was wrong with me? All of a sudden I was blaming a sunflower for all my failings.

What really helped me, what really turned things around, was the girl at the edge of the sidewalk. It took me a second to understand what she was doing. She was moving a worm off the cement.

I stopped next to her and watched. Worms get stranded when it rains. I see them all the time, but who makes the effort to get them safely back to land?

She even had a little stretcher, a slip of yellow paper. She airlifted the worm and laid it to rest in the grass. Then she went back to look for more. This was obviously her thing, to help the world. And she was doing it for free.

I thought about that as I walked along. While I neared the streets and sights of my neighborhood, she stayed in my mind.

I was still thinking of her when I stopped on the corner and went in the laundromat.

I like to imagine this town running on water. There are machineries turning with it, hidden pipes and fountains flowing, and in outposts like this you can see that power up close.

Plastic chairs waited against the wall, facing the rows of washers, each machine with a porthole, the clothes swimming inside like fish lulled by aquarium motors.

There are magazines, a pinball game, the radio is on. When you're here you find things to do. Time itself is counted by how long it takes the water to do its work.

Funny, sometimes you don't even know you're in the right place at the right time until something happens.

That place was waiting for me outside and I would be there in a few minutes. I was in no hurry. I didn't know it would happen yet.

Everyone, even a lover of laundromats, reaches a point where you've seen enough and you're ready to move on. I left midsong.

I seem to know this town in ways only I could. Going back and forth, making it my own. Yesterday there was an eagle in that spot above me. Today it's a seagull.

I still watch the sky for something I lost a while ago. The instructions were so simple:

> Just add water
> to instant crow

So I did and it came to life. Then I don't know where it flew off to. Somewhere in the rain.

It isn't so strange to think that we are also moved by water.

A woman in a long fur coat was waiting for me. A small white dog stood beside her and she held out her hand for money.

I've seen her before. For a long time I thought she could be a character in a book.

You might wonder what sense it makes when someone has to stand in the rain begging and someone else drives by in a car.

I don't know her story. The movie, starring Marlene Dietrich and Clark Gable, steamships, railcars, wit and elegance, was lost years ago.

Supposing I had something she would want, I opened the book and took out a teacup. It was already filled with Darjeeling and I gave it to her.

That was a pretty simple thing to do I know, but I've never seen that for sale.

I walked a little more and stopped. Rain was shining on the ground—the town was a faucet with a leak.

What if the weight of carrying this book full of water was gone? What if these wonders were just here, all around us, everywhere?

It was so simple I almost laughed. Did it really take my whole life to figure that out?

I left a tide pool in a vacant lot. It was a start. I don't know if anyone will find it behind a mattress and an old TV set. Who would expect a starfish hiding back there?

SIMPLE MINDED SUNSHINE

THE RABBIT TELEGRAPH

I wrote most of *Simple Minded Sunshine* in the early morning, in the half hour or so I had before I left for work.

It was a long gray winter and I was thinking of those mysterious rabbit characters: Uncle Wiggly, Br'er Rabbit, Harvey. Spring brings sunshine and rabbits and deer start to appear.

We see them in the woods when I walk the dog, but I also noticed we had a visitor sitting out there while I wrote. Near the end of this book, I looked out the window and saw a rabbit at our doorstep, intent as a telegraph operator. I think that probably explains where this story comes from.

A new day was beginning. The sun shined gold on the wide river. It was warm with the soft colors of a dream and the birds singing, trees sighing and the air full of flowers. Far up in the blue sky went a long chain of geese. They called across the distance. Let it seem like a dream. This might be a place only visited rarely, but it's there. It's there every day and every day begins like this.

A door opened in the side of a grassy hill between two willows. Rabbit stood in the light falling inside and he yawned and stretched and held on to his cane. This was the world he always woke to. Maybe during the night it rained or stormed, but every morning was poured out sweet just like this.

He stepped outside and closed his door and he stood on the soft grass and breathed. Enclosed like a stage set, he lived in a sort of little valley formed by the tall hill to his back, and another steep hill opposite. Between the hills lay a path he mowed every day. The path started at a doorway in a thick hedge wall and ran a hundred feet to the river where a steam engine boat waited. Rabbit didn't have a lot to do besides mowing the path and answering the door when the bell rang in the hedge. And that suited him fine.

Rabbit kept the lawnmower in a hollow tree. That's just where it was and where it belonged. He pulled on the handle and it clacked out. The mechanical sound of its blades fluttered and cut the air. The rabbit's machines, his lawnmower and boat, tried their best to belong, but they were like strange animals here.

The mower stopped and stood there, stork-like, the flowers around it ready to be cut, ready to grow again.

He left his cane at the tree and leaned his weight against the machine, letting it lead him along. It cut the grass and small white daisies on the way to the door in the hedge, turned around and cut a long row down to the river and back again.

When Rabbit was done, there was the path, wide enough for deer walking in pairs. Awaiting their arrival, the path unrolled like carpet from the closed door. After Rabbit shut the mower back in the hollow tree, he followed the path to the river's edge. The steamboat was tied to a short dock.

It felt so good to stand there in the warm sunshine. Sure, the weather was like this every day, but he never tired of the feeling. Eyes closed, he hummed and listened to the pleasant lap of water on the hull of the boat. The cattails played a redwing blackbird song.

Here's something Rabbit never thought about: How did he end up here? And how long had he been here? How long would he stay? There were little flakes of gold in the river, washed in the shallows, brought from somewhere underground he would never know.

A dragonfly landed on the tiller. With nothing else to do it just gleamed. Rabbit rested on his cane the same way. There was one white cloud in the sky, headed for a mountain to curl around.

When it was time to start the boat, he could adjust the lens to heat the boiler and that would turn the propeller. There were others like Rabbit who lived along the river. They had their bells and doors and paths to the water too.

They all had the same simple responsibility: to deliver their boats to the other shore.

Rabbit opened his eyes. The dragonfly was gone, but someone else was nearby, drifting in the river. Rabbit raised his hand and waved. It was his neighbor from the other side of the hill.

Cat was in no rush. Oars stowed halfway, held out like wings, he let the current carry him along. Looking at the trees through his binoculars, Cat purred like a motor getting closer.

"At first, I thought it was a vireo," Cat said. His boat moved slowly past. "But I believe it's a ruby kinglet."

Rabbit looked at the treetops and said he loved it when the birds started the day singing.
Cat nodded, "Yes, the morning chorus."
"They really like it when the sun comes out," Rabbit said. He watched them spark between the branches. Cat's binoculars followed them until his boat disappeared under willow leaves.

With Cat gone, the river gathered itself again and Rabbit felt like sitting down on the dock, maybe with his feet in the water. Rabbits are quite content just sitting.

A breeze swept by: the smell of cut grass, li-lacs, and the muddy banks where the swallows nested. They flew this way and that across the river, low enough to touch.

Rabbit stopped watching the sky when he heard something below. A red windup car bumped into his foot. The tiny voice of Wee Betty called. Her toy car could only take her as far as the river.

After he winded her car, Rabbit turned her around, pointed for the hill. All the ladybugs in the backseat stood and waved as Wee Betty drove away.

Rabbit wondered when the bell would ring and he would have to go open the door. He left the dock and started to follow the path. Bits of cut grass clung to his feet. He had a feeling he would hear the bell any second.

He was right. He almost reached the hedge when it happened. The bell must have been doing this for years. It looked like it had long ago grown from the thick leaves, blossomed from the leaves into a brass flower.

Rabbit unlatched the door and pulled it open. He was looking into darkness, another world at night, a room with no candlelight. Rabbit did what he always did—he stepped to the side and let the sunlight fall in and he made room so the deer could come out.

They never knew where they were, or how they got there, or what would happen. They only flowed through the door and he met them and led them to the water.

This time there were eight deer. Three of them were young and small, still with white dappled spots, the others were older, taller, one with horns you could have hung seven hats on. They waited together in a sort of trance while Rabbit shut the door on the place they had been.

Rabbit didn't need to say a word, they trusted him completely. On either side of the path the stalks of dandelion grew like lampposts.

All the birds were singing. The river, sky, all the greens and blues gentle as a painting. The deer moved in silent clockwork, attached to Rabbit's shadow. He looked like a shepherd bringing them home.

And it was quite a sight to see the steamboat filled with eight deer, but this was normal on the river. There were many other boats too: sailboats, paddlewheels, rowing or barging across. There was even a paper one, folded in neat lines with ants holding on like newsprint.

Rabbit gave the dock a push with his cane and the steamboat chuffed away from land. Several times a day Rabbit became a sailor.

The deer didn't seem to mind. They looked around sleepily, but Rabbit couldn't tell what they were thinking. His boat was just some transport moving them between dreams.

A tin pan full of sparrows floated past. Toad, paddling it, gave Rabbit a quick wave.

This armada of large and small ships were all headed to the same place, the opposite side of the river. It was hidden in thick fog. The sun never showed Rabbit what was there.

Sometimes Rabbit would sing as they crossed. There were plenty of songs about water and the steady beat of the engine parts made an easy melody he knew by heart.

Two horses big as sails on their raft disappeared into the cloud ahead. Soon, Rabbit knew his boat would be in there too.

For lack of sunlight, the steam engine would sputter and cough and Rabbit would have to use an oar to bring them in.

The fog wrapped around the smokestack, the bow, and held to the sides of the boat like hands caught in deer horns.

They didn't have far to go. They had their momentum. Rabbit pushed with the oar and all that white stillness gave way to the sound of sand hushing beneath the hull.

The boat stopped against the shore. Rabbit was the first one overboard, landing in the shallows. He held the boat from rocking while the deer got out, one by one.

They must have known where they were going. Maybe there was some voice calling them that Rabbit couldn't hear. In just a few steps, all eight of them turned into cloud.

Rabbit didn't wonder too much about it. He would return with more deer later. He pushed the boat until the sand gave way and he hopped aboard.

Emerging from the cloud, the river turned sky blue again and Rabbit could restart the steam engine. He readjusted the lens to gather sunshine. How nice to hear it putter into life. He sat at the tiller to steer. He smiled happily. Every ship and floating thing was headed back with him to the sun touched land.

Rabbit tied the boat against the dock. The wake rippled across into the reeds and the shore. With the motor off, he could hear birds again. How much time until he heard the bell and had to ferry more deer? It didn't matter. This is what he did all day.

Rabbit helped twenty one deer across the river before dusk began to fall. Sometimes the number was more, sometimes less. After the last trip, he walked on his long shadow through the grass towards his house in the hill. He was tired and he favored his cane.

It did feel like the days were getting longer, or the sunlight fell on him a little heavier. He went into the ground and shut the door. The wood was warmed and orange with the slow setting glow.

Did the moon appear big in the night sky? Were there stars, owls, bats after moths, did the Milky Way pour like a reflection of the river? Rabbit never knew…he was asleep beneath a pile of blankets.

Usually the sun woke him up. Rabbit would yawn and stretch and rub his eyes and let his cane take him out into the beautiful world opened up before him. This morning was different. Someone was knocking on his door.

It was Turtle. And Rabbit knew it must have taken him a while to crawl all this way from the river.

Turtle was out of breath and his cigarette puffed in the corner of his mouth. "Rabbit!" he wheezed. "Are you still asleep?" This wasn't supposed to happen. Every day started with things to do. The sunny morning air was filled with the birds who always remembered to sing.

Rabbit took a half hop outside and planted his cane to keep from falling. His back was sore today, more than usual. How could he have slept so long? He stared at the hedge with its door and its bell, afraid that he would see a crowd of deer waiting there, ears alert like flowers, eyes shiny as wet river stones.

Turtle shuffled around and said, "I need to ask you a favor. That's the reason I'm here. I left my ducks at the river. My boat is broken down."

Sure enough, there was Turtle's canoe parked on the embankment and Raccoon was bent over the motor taking out parts, tossing them over his shoulder like silver minnows he just caught.

"Where are your ducks?" Rabbit asked. They weren't in the canoe. They weren't on the grass with the engine gears. Turtle slowly pointed towards Rabbit's steamboat.

"You want me to take them across in my boat?" Several boats were out there already. Rabbit could see Cat hoisting a sail. "What if my deer show up while I'm gone?" Cat waved at them as he picked up speed.

"I'll open the door," Turtle said. "I'll be nice to them. I'll keep them company until you get back." He puffed and made a cigarette cloud. Restless ducklings peeped from Rabbit's boat.

That space of water that ran from Rabbit's dock to the foggy bank on the other side and back posed no surprises. No alligators, icebergs, or whirlpools. Time after time he could depend on the swell, the current, weather that was always pleasant. The only difference was Rabbit missed the morning and his deer had been turned into ducks.

Some feathers remained. They wafted in the boat and Rabbit thought about how the hull ground ashore and the way the ducks scampered and flapped to get out. He had to help the little ones, setting them on the sand. They were in such a hurry to get through the reeds, to get lost from sight. Rabbit didn't miss them as much as his deer.

Rabbit could see them from the water—deer placed like statues across the grass, waiting for his approaching steamboat. There was no sign of Turtle, but he couldn't have gone far. His canoe was still there. Worry had never visited here, but now it hung from the nearest tree like a broken window.

Oh, they would all have to be rounded up and gathered into his boat. They were unraveled from each other, spread out like little towns on the prairie, eyes wide, ears cupped to catch another faraway voice. Every one of them watched Rabbit.

It didn't take long to find Turtle. Near the trunk of a tall oak, in a cluster of dandelions and shade, a thin trickle of smoke arose from his shell. Rabbit stopped chasing a fawn and tapped his cane on the dome. "Turtle, are you in there?"

He was, of course. Turtle's head appeared with that cigarette clamped in his mouth and he apologized, "I'm sorry, Rabbit. I tried. I heard the bell and I opened the door, but I'm not used to deer. I didn't know what to do and when I don't like what's going on outside, I just go inside." And with that, he tucked himself back into his shell, leaving only the chimney smoke of his cigarette.

Rabbit would need help funneling the deer into his boat. They were past being slow and somnambulant; they seemed to be feeling quite at home. He opened a cupboard-sized door on a tree and reached for the telephone.

Soon, Rabbit's help arrived, but it took everyone—Blue Jay, Otter, Wee Betty in her car, a hive full of Bumblebees, and Heron—to gather the deer together. Two Butterflies directed a fawn, the last one to get into the boat.

These deer were unlike any Rabbit ever remembered. At times he feared they would jump overboard and it was only the Salmon that kept them from doing so. The fish followed the boat and would rattle the surface if a deer began to lean.

What a voyage it was, and how the deer disappeared like a gust of blossoms when the boat finally hit the foggy shallows. Rabbit got wet pushing the boat off shore. He forgot his cane back on his path, lying somewhere in the crop of new buttercups.

The motor puttered to a stop and once again, as usual, all the birds could be heard. But nobody was there to greet Rabbit—Wee Betty had left, the Butterflies, Bees, Otter, Blue Jay and Heron, and Turtle's canoe was gone.

Rabbit wanted to lie down on the sunny warm planks of the dock. He wanted to look at the water with nothing to do but watch the small fish go slowly from green shadow and travel across the yellow sand.

There was a reason Rabbit walked with a cane and he really needed to find where it was. Time made him tired. He was the hands of a clock, pushing the mower or pointing the boat. That's what he did. Back and forth. He could have done this forever. Funny, he never thought about it until it made him old.

Halfway to the door, Rabbit found his cane where he dropped it during all the deer commotion. It sunned itself like a snake. It had walked with him since he came to this place and maybe in dreams too.

The closest thing to electricity whirred in the air next to Rabbit. Bright as a floating flower, it buzzed like a beautiful idea. Rabbit turned his long ear, but whatever Hummingbird had to say was pitched so high and faraway that Rabbit couldn't hear. A gyroscope running on the perpetual motion of this world's sweetest nectar.

A cloud turned into a comfortable looking armchair. It must have known just what Rabbit wanted. He picked up his cane and looked at the sky again. Thinking about something could turn a cloud into whatever you wished for.

There weren't many shadowy places in this sunny river world. Once, over by the red rhododendron, he lifted a trap door of earth and the worms all shrieked. They wanted to sleep. It was funny to know a whole other world lived side by side, in darkness and night.

The door in the hedge was open just a breath. Did Turtle leave it that way? Rabbit wondered. Then another thought took that one's place: Or had the door opened just that much to keep an eye on him?

Rabbit had to go to the door. He had to pull it open enough to make sure there weren't deer waiting for him. But he held his breath. It was black as underground. The darkness tried to remind him of something he didn't want to remember.

Before Rabbit could shut the door, a bit of black flew out. It went right over his shoulder and landed on a tree branch and swayed and looked at him. It was a crow.

The branch trembled and pointed at the river as the bird hunched and cawed twice. Sometimes crows appeared in the sing-song air but not very often. Its rough voice dropped like ink onto a sheet of music.

Crows could come and go through the door like shadows. Turtle said one time he let nine come through. They stood in a pear tree and watched him shepherd his ducks. From his canoe, Turtle lost sight of their black thread leaving in the sky.

Rabbit turned slowly. Why did he feel so mechanical and worn out?

How long had Rabbit been here, getting up in the morning, walking out of the hill, mowing the path, and delivering deer across the water? And why him? It was such a simple thing, anyone could do it.

The crow wasn't in the tree anymore. The branches were full of green leaves.

There were little white daisies and also a fair number of buttercups tossed around like crumbs on the path. Rabbit gave a moment's thought to getting the push mower out of the hollow tree.

Here's one way of thinking about that door in the hedge that might make sense of its existence. In those long ago days of the late 20th century, skyscrapers were built. Floor after floor stacked on top of each other. Elevators would open and someone would step out as if this other carpeted world was waiting for them to arrive, with clouds outside the window.

As ever, Rabbit gave a startled twitch at the sound of the bell. Raccoon said he could tell before his bell would ring, but that was hard to believe. From the river, Rabbit had seen Raccoon scurry across the length of his yard, balled up in a rush like a crumpled piece of paper.

So it was back to the routine, to open the door and let the deer out and lead them in a sleepy line towards the steamboat waiting in the water. Or so Rabbit thought.

Whatever he was expecting—a doorway filled with his next passengers and the solemn passage of them into the fog—didn't happen. The door opened by itself and another Rabbit appeared.

Seeing her brought back memories he forgot. He remembered being that young and he remembered coming here and he knew what would happen next. She was here to take his place.

He pointed out her new home in the hill (she could soon make that her own) and as they walked he showed her the lawnmower's tree. He apologized for the flowers on the path. He never had time to get to that. It didn't really matter now.

The river sparked with a thousand pieces of sun as Rabbit explained how the steam engine ran. She understood—it was easy for her—and soon they started across the bright water. She steered them towards the clouds. They both knew only one of them was coming back.

Allen Frost has published 22 books of poetry, fiction and biography. He lives with his family by the inland sea.

Laura Vasyutynska is an accomplished visual artist who has been pursuing a career as a professional artist since her youth, beginning formal training in her hometown of Zhytomyr, Ukraine. Laura moved to the United States in early 2001 and continued her career in Seattle. A former student at Western Washington University. She works primarily with oils on canvas, but also uses other media such as watercolors and graphite. www.vlaura.com
Laura previously illustrated Allen's sci-fi book, *Different Planet*.

HOMELESS SUTRA
written by Allen Frost

Homeless Sutra: 9/25/16—12/30/16
Mountain Temple: 2/1/17—2/14/17
Instant Crow: 2/21/17—3/16/17
Simple Minded Sunshine: 4/25/17—5/23/17

Books by Good Deed Rain

Saint Lemonade, Allen Frost, 2014. Two novels illustrated by the author in the manner of the old Big Little Books.

Playground, Allen Frost, 2014. Poems collected from seven years of chapbooks.

Roosevelt, Allen Frost, 2015. A Pacific Northwest novel set in July, 1942, when a boy and a girl search for a missing elephant. Illustrated throughout by Fred Sodt.

5 Novels, Allen Frost, 2015. Novels written over five years, featuring circus giants, clockwork animals, detectives and time travelers.

The Sylvan Moore Show, Allen Frost, 2015. A short story omnibus of 193 stories written over 30 years.

Town in a Cloud, Allen Frost, 2015. A three-part book of poetry, written during the Bellingham rainy seasons of fall, winter, and spring.

A Flutter of Birds Passing Through Heaven: A Tribute to Robert Sund. 2016. Edited by Allen Frost and Paul Piper. The story of a legendary Ish River poet & artist.

At the Edge of America, Allen Frost, 2016. Two novels in one book blend time travel in a mythical poetic America.

Lake Erie Submarine, Allen Frost, 2016. A two week vacation in Ohio inspired these poems, illustrated by the author.

and Light, Paul Piper, 2016. Poetry written over three years. Illustrated with watercolors by Penny Piper.

The Book of Ticks, Allen Frost, 2017. A giant collection of 8 mysterious adventures featuring Phil Ticks. Illustrated throughout by Aaron Gunderson.

I Can Only Imagine, Allen Frost, 2017. Five adventures of love and heartbreak dreamed in an imaginary world. Cover & color illustrations by Annabelle Barrett.

The Orphanage of Abandoned Teenagers, Allen Frost, 2017. A fictional guide for teens and their parents. Illustrated by the author.

In the Valley of Mystic Light: An Oral History of the Skagit Valley Arts Scene, 2017. Edited by Claire Swedberg & Rita Hupy.

Different Planet, Allen Frost, 2017. Four science fiction adventures: reincarnation, robots, talking animals, outer space and clones. Cover & illustrations by Laura Vasyutynska.

Go with the Flow: A Tribute to Clyde Sanborn. 2018. Edited by Allen Frost. The life and art of a timeless river poet.

Homeless Sutra, Allen Frost, 2018. Four stories: Sylvan Moore, a flying monk, a water salesman, and a guardian rabbit.

Coming soon:

A Hundred Dreams Ago, Allen Frost, 2018. A winter book of poetry and prose.

good deed rain

www.ingramcontent.com/pod-product-compliance
Lightning Source LLC
Chambersburg PA
CBHW020010140726
47904CB00018B/2197

* 9 7 8 1 6 4 2 0 4 5 4 0 6 *